THE SOAK

THE SOAK

PATRICK MCLEAN

The characters and events portrayed in this book are fictitious. Any similarity to real persons, living or dead, is coincidental and not intended by the author.

ISBN: 0997832312
ISBN-13: 9780997832310

Published by Brash Books, LLC
12120 State Line #253,
Leawood, Kansas 66209

www.brash-books.com

PART ONE
MEAN OLD MAN

ONE

Three months after

"Hey, the dead guy woke up."

These were not words Hobbs had expected to hear. He had not expected to hear anything ever again. He was supposed to be dead, and he felt as if he were.

He opened his eyes and regretted it. He saw that he was in a windowless room like a hospital room, but dirtier and more lived in. There was a mirror on the other side of the room, and in it he could see a skull draped in skin peering over the edge of the plastic footboard. He was used to being on the far side of sixty, but that thing floating in the mirror looked to be on the far side of death. He turned away from himself and winced at the pain of it.

In the bed to his right was a fat, round-faced, old man with an idiot's leer and an oxygen tube in his nose. To his left was the door. Hobbs had no urge to punch the door.

"Hi there, roomie, have a nice nap?"

Hobbs didn't answer. He leaned to the left and tried to get out of bed. Pain and nausea overcame him. "Water," he said. Then he lay back on the bed, drained.

He closed his eyes and heard his roommate say, "They don't really have room service here."

Then he passed out.

The next time he woke up, someone was shaking his shoulder. "C'mon, buddy. Wake up there."

Hobbs opened his eyes. A young man in shabby clothing presented some credentials and said, "I'm Mr. Upshaw, the social worker assigned to your case. What's your name?"

Hobbs asked, "What am I doing here? What is this place?"

"This is the Clover Street Senior Living Facility, if you call this living." He flipped through his paperwork. "You were found wadded up behind a Dumpster, with two gunshot wounds, about an inch and a half away from death. You were treated, but when they couldn't get you out of a coma—or find anybody to claim you—they parked you here. Shady Acres. That's all I got. What's your side?" The man closed his mouth and looked at Hobbs. Hobbs wondered if this was his strong-arm technique.

Hobbs reached for the plastic pitcher of water on the nightstand and drank from it. When he had drained it, he set it back down, trying not to let his hand shake. He sighed.

"Nothing?" said the social worker. "You give me nothing? What did I drive all the way out here for?"

"I don't remember anything."

"Really? That's your story? You mean amnesia, like in a bad TV show?"

Hobbs looked at him.

"You wake up from a coma that nobody thought you would come out of—"

"I was prayin' for him. I knew Jesus wouldn't let him down," interjected the roommate.

The social worker continued, having had lots of practice ignoring crazy people, "—so I'd say you've got something worth living for. Something pretty important. Not the kind of thing you forget. Looks like somebody tried to kill you. And mister, you're old. You look so old, that if I had a beef with you, I'd just let time settle the score. But somebody wanted you dead in a hurry. You want to tell me anything about that? About why you want to live so bad?"

Hobbs stared at the social worker. He said, "Livin'? You come lay down in this bed and you tell me that the view doesn't look like hell."

The roommate piped up again. "Accept Jesus Christ as your Lord and Savior and ye need not fear even the Fires of Hell." As he recited this verse from Imbeciles 21:13, spit flew from his lips with the words *fear* and *fires*.

Hobbs said, "See?"

He closed his eyes and heard the social worker say, "I can't help you if you don't help me. And the cops don't want to help you at all."

Hobbs fell asleep. The next time he woke up, the social worker was gone.

Over the next week, a little of his strength returned. But when he used his wheelchair as a walker, he felt as if someone had smashed a pint glass and stitched it into his stomach.

"Easy, friend," said the roommate, taking his eyes off the TV to watch Hobbs struggle. "It's a rest home, after all."

Every time Hobbs lay back down in the bed, he was afraid he would never be able to get out again.

By the end of the second week, Hobbs felt well enough to reconnoiter. No cops had shown up to question him, and why should they? As far as they knew he was just another John Doe. A nobody. They didn't know who he was, where he had been, or what he had done. They'd gotten his prints, but that wouldn't get them anywhere. Maybe they'd get a juvie hit from California all those years ago, but that was under another name, and he doubted those prints would be in any computer. He marveled to think it, but that was the last time anybody had put the pinch on him.

By the time anybody got around to checking up on him, he would already be gone. The only question was how.

TWO

First Hobbs tried to walk out. Glimpses out the dirty windows revealed that he was on the fourth or fifth floor of whatever building he was in. The doors to the stairwells were locked and alarmed. But it didn't matter. He couldn't manage five flights of stairs in his condition.

The elevators were in the center of the floor, behind a door that the staff had to use keycards to get through. This was a minimum-security prison for geriatrics. Hobbs was locked in here with the rest of the feeble, washed-out, discarded people.

The coffee tasted like burnt piss. The food, regardless of the color, all had the same pasty texture and the same vague aftertaste of stale oatmeal.

He watched the security door from the cafeteria area for two days before he tried to make it through to the elevators. He was still using the wheelchair as a walker, but it was an act. He didn't feel whole, but he thought he could move without it. He hadn't tested how far, but he was certain he was getting better.

So when a white-haired inmate stood up, pulled her shirt over her head, and started screaming about "secret Martian niggers" coming to rape her, it was just the distraction he was looking for. The staff rushed to contain her, including the nurse from the front desk.

When she passed, Hobbs got up a little too quickly. There was a twinge in his stomach, and a sharp pain. He broke out in a sweat, but pressed on. One foot in front of the other, quickly, but not looking as if he was in a hurry. He walked directly to the nurses' station, without looking back.

Inside, he rifled through several of the drawers, looking for a magnetic pass card, but came up empty. Then he took a chance and leaned down to peer under the desk. As his head swam, he saw the well-worn button that opened the magnetic lock on the main door. He stood up again, and held on to the counter as the floor pitched underneath him. Maybe he had been too ambitious. Jesus Christ, bending over without passing out was an ambition now?

He stood there trying not to throw up. The underpaid, overworked Jamaican nurse appeared in the doorway.

"What are you doin' in here?"

"I was scared," he said, shocked to find that it was true. He had never thought about getting old—well, maybe old, but never infirm. He was a little over sixty and had thought he had years before he needed to worry about being out of breath while climbing stairs, or about turning forgetful or anything like that. But here he was, surrounded by the walking dead, old before his time. Needing to save himself and unable.

He knew men didn't cry, but right now he had the urge.

"Don't let the crazy woman worry you none, handsome," said the nurse, seeing the distress on Hobbs's face. "She just a mean ol' wo-man."

"You really a Martian?" Hobbs asked with a wan smile. She chuckled and shooed him away.

That night, after lights-out, Hobbs got out of bed and opened the room door. He looked out into the hallway.

The roommate said, "Oh no, you don't want to do that. Mr. Ray is on tonight. You don't want to mess with Mr. Ray. He hurts you if you don't behave."

"Go back to sleep," said Hobbs.

"He that seeketh evil, it shall come unto him," said the roommate, adding, "Proverbs," as an apology and explanation all in one.

Hobbs thought, *Even when you don't seeketh, evil comes anyway.*

Mr. Ray was a night nurse with something to prove, a bully of the worst kind, who preyed on the defenselessness of the elderly. A lot of people in here weren't even lucid enough to remember that they should be afraid of him.

A few days ago Mr. Ray had introduced himself by coming down on Hobbs. Hobbs had been watching the shift change at the end of the day, and shuffled into the nurses' station to get a cup of coffee.

"Yo, grandpa. The hell you think you're doing?" Mr. Ray barked.

Hobbs didn't look at him. He knew that baiting this guy was a bad idea, but he didn't care. He'd been here too long and was going stir-crazy. Besides, what was this clown going to do? Inside, this bully nurse had to be a coward.

Hobbs grabbed a cup in a shaky hand and poured some coffee. When he turned, there was Mr. Ray, red faced and sputtering. Hobbs took a sip and looked at him.

He saw the slap coming, but couldn't move fast enough to get out of the way. Mr. Ray's meaty palm slammed into Hobbs's ear and the side of his face. As Hobbs clung to the counter and struggled to keep his feet underneath him, the ringing started in his ears.

Mr. Ray looked down at where coffee was splattered on his scrubs. The wet stains called attention to the fact that the big man was running to fat as if it were a race he meant to win. The pressure built inside Mr. Ray and his face grew redder. He leaned in to Hobbs and spoke quickly and softly. Hobbs turned his deaf ear to him, hoping that the ringing would drown out this guy's bullshit. It didn't.

"Old man, you know who I am? I am *Mister* Ray. You try that shit again, I will slap the wrinkles off of you. Now get back to your room while I am still in a charitable frame of mind."

Hobbs had to hold a hand to the wound in his leg to straighten up. To weakness and shakiness he now added a sharp pain. With effort Hobbs stood and looked Mr. Ray in the eye. The nurse was mad, but not mad enough. Not yet. Over his shoulder he saw the head nurse coming back from her rounds. Maybe this would be the play. Or, at least, the play before the play.

Hobbs spit in Mr. Ray's face.

It almost got Mr. Ray to pop. But he was a smart, institutional bully. He wiped the spit off his face just as the nurse supervisor said, "What's going on here?"

Mr. Ray turned around, sweet as a Valentine's Day card, and said, "Mr. Doe has gotten a little confused. I was just taking him back to his room."

"This area is for staff only, Mr. Doe," the nurse supervisor said, in the same tone of voice she would use for a three-year-old. Hobbs nodded.

Mr. Ray took Hobbs's arm and guided him down the hallway. As soon as they were out of earshot, Mr. Ray whispered. "You're gonna pay for that, grandpa."

"I don't have any kids."

"Shut your wrinkle hole. I'm gonna come for you, sometime in the middle of the night. Maybe tonight, maybe tomorrow night, maybe next week, but soon. I'm gonna fuckin' kill you, man. Sooner or later, maybe just slip a needle in your IV and give you a little something-something. Maybe just an air bubble the size of my dick, you know. Whatever it is, ain't nobody gonna care. You wouldn't be up in here if you had some people to care for you. Shit, nobody would. So who's gonna investigate me? Who's gonna care one ol' cracka strokes out in the middle of the night?

"Beside, don't nobody believe that John Doe bullshit. Wheeling you in here with a GSW in your gut and that withered-up ol' leg. Who knows what bad shit you done? Maybe I be doing the world a favor. Maybe I be doing you a favor. Maybe the cops be the least of your worries, your former associates likewise, 'cause now you on the wrong side of Mr. Ray Ray."

As he spoke, Mr. Ray squeezed Hobbs's arm harder and harder. But when Mr. Ray looked for fear and pain on Hobbs's face, he could find none.

"Don't matter how tough you act. You know old people doze off, grandpa? You gotta sleep sometime," Mr. Ray said, giving Hobbs a shove into his room that caused him to stagger and grab for the railing on the wall.

Mr. Ray raised his voice so it would carry all the way back to the nurses' station. "You sleep tight, Mr. Doe."

Hobbs staggered into the bathroom and closed the door. He lowered himself onto the toilet riser, an industrial steel-and-plastic contraption that lifted the toilet seat to a height that the infirm could more easily manage. It was old and yellowed and cracked. The plastic screeched under his weight as he sat down.

Hobbs sat there for a moment, catching his breath, then stood and dropped his pants. He checked the puckered scars to the right of his belly button and on the front of his left thigh. The doctors had said the leg wound was lucky. The bullet had gone in, grazed the bone, and passed through. Lucky? He felt as if someone had filled his hip joint with cold sand. And he was weak, so weak. He sat on the toilet again. He cursed as the plastic moved and pinched his ass. A millimeter of skin caught in a tiny crack on the side of the seat hurt so badly that it brought tears to his eyes.

Was this to be the end of it? The end of him? Was this the way he would go out? It had all been in his hands, and that bitch had taken it away from him. From all of them.

He reached down and grabbed the side of the aged plastic. With all the strength he could muster, he pulled up. He groaned, he strained, and then, with a crack, a long, sharp piece of plastic came free. He put the point against the wall and pressed. It bent, but didn't break.

When he climbed back into bed, the roommate said, "I warned you not to mess with Mr. Ray."

THREE

Four hours later he heard a faint jingling of keys. Mr. Ray was coming down the hallway. The man's comfortable shoes made no sound, but the keys on his belt loop, softly clinking together, made just enough noise to give him away.

Hobbs had lain in his bed patiently, waiting as a professional does. Not waiting for something to happen, not even wanting something to happen, just watching and listening for what did happen.

Hobbs looked over and saw the wide eyes of the roommate looking at him. Hobbs said, "Turn the other cheek. Pretend to be asleep." The roommate did not look away. *Suit yourself*, thought Hobbs. He heard Mr. Ray shutting the door of the room and trying to be quiet about it. Hobbs closed his eyes.

This was the hard part.

He heard the footsteps grow closer to the bed and fought a battle not to flinch from an imagined blow he couldn't see. Hobbs needed the man close. Even though Mr. Ray was a fat, greasy shit, Hobbs was in no condition to run him down. He'd get one shot. If he could get him close.

He smelled bad cologne, and felt the man's breath in his ear as he said, "I can kill you whenever I please, but not today."

Hobbs opened his eyes.

Mr. Ray said, "Yeah, that's right…"

Hobbs turned quickly in the bed and drove the plastic into Mr. Ray's kidney. Ray's face, an inch from his, lost all color. His mouth made a large, round circle, but no sound escaped. Mr. Ray tried to breathe in and failed. He clawed at the side of the bed and then collapsed in a heap along the wall.

Hobbs threw the bedclothes to the other side and regained his feet.

"You're going to hell," whispered the roommate.

Hobbs snapped the keycard off Mr. Ray's belt with a brutal jerk. "Not tonight."

The roommate looked at Hobbs with wide eyes and shook his jowls as if the momentum could make the whole thing a bad dream. Hobbs knew that the roommate was going to scream before the fat man realized it himself. Hobbs rolled across his bed and staggered to his feet. The roommate sucked in air to scream. Hobbs got to him before he could let it out.

Mr. Ray's scrubs were too big for Hobbs. He cuffed the pants and tucked the shirt in as best he could. He tore his hospital gown in half and stuffed half into each of the nurse's shoes. They were uncomfortable, but they stayed on his feet.

Hobbs walked calmly past the nurses' station without looking. The trick to doing something wrong and getting away with it was to do it as if you did it all the time. Hobbs flashed the card at the sensor and pushed through the doors into the elevator lobby. He pressed the button and looked around as though he were bored. Only then did he risk a glance at the nurses' station. It was empty.

In the parking lot, he found Mr. Ray's car by walking around and clicking the key fob until he heard a chirp. It was a beat-up Pontiac Firebird with an aftermarket alarm system and a plastic scrotum and balls dangling from the rear bumper. Big nuts with nothing to back them up. Hobbs thought that summed up Mr. Ray's life in a nutshell. And then he never thought of him again.

The majority of the cars in the lot had North Carolina license plates on them. He had made it that far north? He was tougher than he'd thought. Tougher than he felt for sure. He really didn't remember much of the end of it. Inside the car he checked Mr. Ray's wallet and saw that his address was indeed in Charlotte, North Carolina. It had been years, nearly thirty, since he had been here. And he didn't remember much about that either. Just a payroll job at a mill on the north end of town that he had bailed out of when it had gone wrong.

He smiled. Maybe that job could come to something good after all these years. A plan began to take shape in his head. He felt weak, but good. He went through the glove box and checked under and behind the seats. No firearms. No cell phone. All clear. He had 120 dollars in cash from Mr. Ray's wallet, and he figured he had until morning, if his luck held, before word was out on the Firebird.

Cameras would make him leaving the nasty five-story Brutalist building he had just escaped from. Rest home? Hobbs snorted. He turned the engine and the headlights leapt across the badly kept lawn. That was a prison. A slow-motion death row with no appeals. Better to be hunted than to be caged.

FOUR

Detective Mazerick looked at the crime scene and couldn't stop chuckling. The nursing home administrator hovered outside the door and shot Mazerick a dirty look every time he snickered, but Mazerick couldn't stop himself. And why should he care about that dink? He didn't know what it was like to be murder police. He especially didn't know what it was like to have your partner catch it. Not from a shootout or cancer or any dramatic TV bullshit like that. Nope, just running a red light while drunk and getting T-boned by a Caddy.

All well and good for Jimson, his troubles had come to an end. Mazerick was the one who was left behind, still holding down a full caseload, one man doing the work of two until a suitable replacement could be found. He was buried in the grind of a job that would burn people out with an ordinary caseload. So Mazerick took his yuks where he could get them. And *this*? This was *funny.*

He chuckled again and heard the administrator sigh with exasperation. That made him chuckle some more. It was a grim sense of humor that kept you going in this job.

He sucked his teeth and asked the uniformed cop at the door, "You ever hear of anybody breaking out of a rest home before?"

The cop shook his head.

"Can you blame him?" Mazerick asked.

The cop shook his head again.

"You ever want to make detective?" Mazerick asked. The uniform, a young kid with a shaved head, nodded. Of course he did. "Then step in here and help me talk this through."

The uniform asked, "What happened to your partner?"

"See that, a natural detective—he had an accident. I just need somebody to talk at, so, you know...shut up. OK, so Mr. Doe, former occupant of this bed, is brought here in a coma, three weeks ago. Severely dehydrated, two gunshot wounds, a concussion, and injuries consistent with a"—here he flipped open the file and read—"vigorous physical beating."

"Who'd he piss off?" asked the uniform.

"*Whom*, had to be multiple guys—the GSWs were already treated when he was picked up...behind a Dumpster behind a Bojangles on South Tryon."

"*Who* is a plural."

"What?" said Mazerick, looking up from the file.

"*Who* or *whom* doesn't make a difference."

"Seriously, you're correcting my grammar? That's just obnoxious. It's not going to help you rise in the ranks, that's for sure." He turned back to the empty bed. "So our guy, who is evidently popular with a range of unknown persons, wakes up from his coma, takes a few days to get his legs under him. Then kills a nurse and escapes."

"What about the guy in the other bed?" the uniform asked.

"I questioned him downstairs in the clinic. But it's a pain in the ass to get information out of a guy with a broken jaw. Says he saw the guy kill the nurse, but other than that he doesn't know anything. Except that Mr. Doe was the devil and he was most certainly going to hell."

"Why doesn't Mr. Doe just walk out?" asked the uniform.

"Good question, wrong question, but a good question. He doesn't just walk out because they won't let him. But the better question is, why doesn't he just stay?"

"What?"

"Kick back, enjoy the Ensure, rest and heal. Why is he in such a hurry?"

Mazerick looked at the room again to give the uniform time to figure it out.

"Somebody was after him!" said the uniform.

"That's one," said Mazerick. "What's the other one?" This time Mazerick waited so long, he ran out of patience. So he answered his own question: "Or he was after somebody or something and was worried about running out of time."

"He could just be angry," offered the uniform.

Mazerick squinted and waggled his open hand from side to side. "Kinda weak."

"So who is this old boy?"

"Yeah," said Mazerick, "that's the thing. Who is this guy? And right now we don't know. And we've got no way of knowing. All we got is a stolen car maybe six hours old, some prints that don't match anything, some pictures, and some shitty surveillance cam footage. Unless he's stupid and we catch him, we may never know who he is or what he wants."

A female voice from the doorway said, "I know who he is."

Mazerick and the uniform turned to see a woman in a dark-blue suit. Mazerick immediately thought, *Naughty librarian.* And a split second after, he thought, *There goes that sensitivity training the city paid for.* Screw them, this lady was one of those suits who managed to turn the line between professional and sexy into a demilitarized zone—a place where you knew action should happen, but if it ever did, you just knew that shit would be going all the way wrong.

Thick blond hair, white blouse straining to hold its contents in, dark-red nail polish, and, at the very end, the badge and ID wallet that read "FBI." He tried not to let his biological reaction show; that was just a sure way to piss off a broad like this. And he had an overwhelming urge to try to make her happy.

"Great," said Mazerick, "but who are you?"

"Special Agent Wellsley, FBI," she said. Mazerick loved the way she pronounced all three syllables. *F-B-I*, her upper teeth pinning her lower lip as she enunciated the *F*.

"FBI," joked Mazerick. "You gonna take over this domestic rest home terrorist case? Snatch this nurse murder from my plate?"

"Actually," Agent Wellsley said, displaying a humility that Mazerick had not expected from an FBI agent, "I was hoping for a little cooperation."

"Yeah, sure," said Mazerick, "but by the time I'm done, we'll probably have him in the bag. He's a feeble old man, we got the car he's driving, he doesn't have any credit cards. He's gonna leave a trail like he's dropping glowing bread crumbs."

"I hope you're right, Detective..."

"Mazerick, ma'am."

"Ma'am?" asked Wellsley, playing at being offended.

"Eh, sorry, I moved down here from New York a few years back, it just kinda rubbed off."

Agent Wellsley smiled. Mazerick liked it.

FIVE

Hobbs had started north on little more than instinct. When he saw signs for the interstate, he jumped on the superslab. It was forty-five minutes of drone and wind before he saw what he was looking for. It came in the form of a train station. At four forty-five in the morning he pulled into the Amtrak parking lot in Salisbury, North Carolina. He eased the Firebird into a spot in the back and killed the engine. There weren't many lights in the lot, and back here the illumination came from a couple of old-fashioned frosted globe streetlights with a tree growing around them. Hobbs sat in the darkness until his eyes adjusted.

He had to fight off the urge to sleep. He knew he sorely needed it. But he needed to make one more move before he could rest for a while. Still, he felt fatigue pulling him down. When one eye drooped, he snapped upright in his seat, asking himself, "You want to rest in jail?"

He scanned the lot until he found something that would work. Four spots over, an ancient but well-loved pickup truck. *Ancient*, thought Hobbs. He remembered when that model was new. It was back when he was new. He reached up and clawed the plastic dome off the Firebird's cabin light. Then he pulled out the bulb so he wouldn't call attention to himself or ruin his night vision when he opened the door.

He got out of the car and groaned with the effort of unfolding. He stepped into the landscaped median that separated the rows of parking spaces. He stood motionless in the shadows. The only thing he could hear in this town was his breathing. Then he heard the stoplight change on Main Street.

He saw a light play across the storefronts on the far side of the street. Then he fell down. He had meant to kneel gently by one of the trees, but there was a pain and his leg gave out. He heard something crack and hoped it was just one of his old joints.

It was bad to move fast. The eye is attracted to fast-moving things, especially in low light. Nothing for it now. So he lay on the ground and watched the police car glide past. Was it looking for something in particular? Couldn't be. Sure they had to have him on cameras, but had they gotten the word out that fast? He was sixty miles away. They couldn't have gotten the word out that fast. But, as Hobbs slowed and aged, there seemed to be no limit to how fast everything around him became.

The police car disappeared at the far end of the street. Hobbs decided the cop was just bored and on a regular patrol.

He got up slowly and it hurt. He limped to the old truck and tried the driver's side door. Locked. Then he pressed his hand against the window and slid it down. Old truck meant old parts. Old parts meant that sometimes there was enough play in the window that it would slide down and give him the space to reach in and pull the door lock. But not this one. Then he tried the triangular little window at the front of the door, but it didn't budge either.

Hobbs worked his way around to the passenger side, stopping to feel the top of each tire and the well under the rear bumper. He came up empty, but then he tried the window trick on the passenger window and it slid down about three inches. He worked his hand and arm through the door, then pulled up on the lock mechanism. The door was well greased and opened without a sound. Somebody was going to miss this truck.

He switched off the interior light and waited. He thought he heard something, so he pulled his head out of the pickup and listened for a long time. A sharp pain went through his skull, reminding him that he was tired, too tired. There wasn't even wind. The air on this hot Southern night just hung in place and sweated.

He leaned into the car and reached underneath the dash and made a sharp jerk. He came up with three wires. He squinted at them for a second, but couldn't make out the colors. He stripped them, one at a time, with his teeth, making sure not to ground himself against any of the metal in the mostly metal cab. After everything he'd been through, there was no need to take twelve volts in the mouth. When he had them stripped, he cupped the overhead light and turned it back on. He needed only a sliver to see which wire was which.

He slid in behind the wheel and closed the passenger side door behind him quietly. He wondered, wait for the cop to pass again, or chance it? Better to be active than passive. Besides, if he were that cop he'd be asleep somewhere by now.

Before he touched the wires together, he felt around and found the manual choke knob. It wouldn't need much on a hot night like tonight, but a little wouldn't hurt. He pulled it out halfway. Then he twisted the red and the blue wires together. When he touched the black to them, the engine sputtered and tried to start. He gave it a little gas and the good old truck turned right over and purred.

He dropped the column shift into place and eased it out of the lot. There was a lot of life left in this old truck, and for the first time since he'd woken up in that rest home, he felt some hope for the future.

As he merged onto I-85 again, this time headed south, he flipped open the triangular window in the front of the door and let the air rush across him. He chuckled an evil, phlegmy, old-man chuckle. Yeah, he thought, a nap and a couple more good moves, and he'd be back on the right side of this thing.

SIX

It took Mazerick and Wellsley less than twenty-four hours to find the dead nurse's Firebird. By the time the two of them were looking through the video surveillance footage from the Amtrak station in Salisbury, North Carolina, Wellsley had learned more about Detective Mazerick than she had ever wanted to know.

She had had to tell him about her partner. Not the whole truth about Barry, of course. But enough to explain why she was in a rental car. Why she was on "administrative leave." Why she didn't have the full might of the FBI behind her. She put tears in her eyes when she told him the part about working the case on her own because she needed to redeem herself. Because she needed to make it right for her dead partner.

The flabby fuck ate it up with a spoon. *Jesus Christ*, thought Wellsley, between the time "Sleeping Beauty" had been written and the present day, not a damn thing had changed. Not one damn thing. She didn't let the anger show. And wasn't that the best kind of feminism—making all this bullshit work for you? She wasn't going to waste too much time thinking about it. There was more at stake here than some transplanted prick from New York.

She knew everything she needed to know about Mazerick when he picked her up in the hotel lobby. At the rest home he had been wearing a wedding ring. As they headed north, he wasn't. The guy had no idea he was a caricature of himself. *Means to an end*, she kept telling herself, *he's a means to an end.*

They set up in a back office of the train station, where the security footage was located. On the monitor they had playback—agonizingly slow even at double speed—of the main lobby camera. A tech with a ratty neck beard was copying the video surveillance drives to a laptop.

"So," said Mazerick, managing to piss her off with a single syllable, "first train was seven forty-three, northbound Carolinian. Nobody matching his description bought a ticket. I got techs watching the footage, but I'm betting he didn't get on the train. So why was he here?"

"Do we have footage of the parking lot?"

"Not IR, too dark to see anything," said the shaggy tech.

"What about the afternoon before?"

"What do you mean, the afternoon before? You mean before he escaped?" asked Mazerick.

"Yes," said Wellsley. "Can you bring it up?"

The tech shrugged. Of course he could bring it up. Was he not an elder of the neck beard tribe? One of the elite whom computers feared and recognized as their master? A few keystrokes and a window popped up. On the screen they saw a parking lot shimmering in the heat of a July day. A yellow dog, tongue hanging out, trotted from one shadow to another, knowing enough not to directly cross the expanse of blacktop.

"Pause it," said Wellsley, her voice stern. She looked at the frozen image for a moment.

"You know that dog?" Mazerick joked.

She left the room.

"Where's she going?" Mazerick asked the neck beard. The tech answered with a jowly shrug. "She's pretty hot, though, right?" Mazerick asked.

Without looking up the neck beard said, "She's gonna put your nuts in a vise."

"Rowr," said Mazerick.

"That's not a good thing," the neck beard muttered. He turned his attention back to the computers. He liked them better anyway. They were productive and reasonable.

Wellsley came back into the room and scrutinized the picture again.

"Special Agent," said Mazerick, "would you mind clueing the rest of us mere mortals in?"

She pointed to an old powder-blue F-100 pickup truck on the screen. "I think he stole that truck."

"Hey, don't touch the screen," the tech said, defensive of his equipment.

"I want you to watch the footage for the truck. Tell me when somebody drives it off."

"So he drove all the way up here, to a train station, to steal a truck?" asked Mazerick.

"That's right. Long-term airport parking lots used to be the best place for this kind of thing. Vehicles won't be reported stolen for a while. He's buying time."

"Well, at least now we know he's headed north," said Mazerick.

SEVEN

He parked the truck behind a church and slept for a while. By nine thirty the heat of the day woke him. He was dry and hungry and his joints didn't want to move.

He stopped at an old convenience store and got coffee, water, a map, and a vile-tasting microwaved breakfast sandwich. It was a mom-and-pop place in a bad neighborhood. It had once sold gas, but the pumps had been removed. The place did a brisk trade in lottery tickets and the holy trinity of the convenience store: condoms, smokes, and beer.

As he laid the map on the counter, the light-brown clerk said in a singsong accent, "Map? You don't have a smartphone?"

Hobbs just shook his head and kept it turned away from the camera behind the plexiglass shield. "No, too smart for me."

Back in the truck he looked at the map and ate the sandwich. He wondered if it would still be there. Only one way to find out. He started the truck. Its throaty, big-engined rumble was reassuring. He would be sad to part with it.

The neighborhood he was looking for had changed since the last time Hobbs had been there. After ripping off that textile mill payroll, he had never wanted to see this place again. Now that he had come back, he realized that he never would. Everything had changed.

The city had flourished, and this neighborhood of rundown mill houses on the north side of a booming city center had been gentrified. The mills here had been converted to high-end apartments. The theater that had showed porn now booked bluegrass acts. The whorehouse had been converted into a pizza joint. The artists who had moved in for the cheap living had painted the drab houses all kinds of crazy colors, then sold them to yuppies, the kind of people who had to buy their cool at full retail. Later these yuppies had knocked the colorful houses down and built new ones on top of the ruins. It was now a neighborhood of people who went antiquing. It made Hobbs feel like an antique.

The house he was looking for was still there. It had been a shotgun shack. Now it was a two-story shotgun shack, with big windows and a fresh coat of lavender paint. He didn't need to go inside to know that the place had granite countertops.

He parked the truck down the street in the shade and watched the house. A guy came out on the front porch with a phone and a laptop. He spent a lot of time on the phone, and he talked with his hands.

After two hours of this, Hobbs realized this guy wasn't going to leave. In the old days he would have waited it out. Patience was a heister's best tool. The heavier the hit, the more of it you needed. But he had lost too much time. They'd make this truck sooner or later. As if to prove the point, he saw a patrol car sliding along underneath the shadows of the oak trees on the next street over. Always a cop when you didn't need one.

He stepped out of the Ford and shut the door behind him. On the porch the yuppie was shifting his attention back and forth between the laptop screen and the smartphone, typing on one, texting on the other. Hobbs's legs shook as he walked. He told himself he was just playing the part of a frail old man.

The yuppie didn't even look up until Hobbs was on the porch, and then he held up a finger as if to say, "Lemme just finish typing this."

Hobbs said, "My truck broke down, and I'd like to use your phone to call a..."

The yuppie looked up and evaluated the person he saw in front of him, and then an expression of concern crossed his face. "Of course," he said. Hobbs realized his mistake even as the yuppie swiped the code on his smartphone. He handed it to Hobbs. Hobbs just stared at it. "Do you, uh, know how to use that?" the yuppie asked.

Fuck it. "I don't really need your phone." That got the yuppie's attention, but he wasn't yet afraid. Hobbs had been physically threatening all his life, so he wasn't sure how to play it when he wasn't. It was hard to grow old and learn new ways to do the old, old things. Maybe that's why people retired?

"I'll tell you the truth. My bladder is the size of a walnut. And I gotta take a leak, or I'm gonna whiz in my truck over there. So, I was wondering," he said, putting all his limited acting skills into it. "If I could use your head."

The yuppie's frown faded away into an understanding smile. "Same thing happened to my grandfather, toward the end. You should have heard him complain about it on fishing trips. C'mon inside," he said, leading the way.

Hobbs let him get in the door, then he dropped the heel of his fist into the back of the yuppie's neck. It was a good shot, and the yup dropped like a sack. Looking at him in a heap on the floor, Hobbs didn't feel so old and worn out. Then he realized that his bladder really was small, and he really did have to pee.

After, in the bathroom, he splashed water on his face and neck. When he was done patting his face down with a towel, he looked at it in the mirror and realized that, for some reason, the vain, unconscious fucker who owned this house had put up facing mirrors. So you could see all of yourself, and infinity, if you looked the right way.

He saw the number eleven on the back of his neck. The two tendons, standing up away from the skin and the muscle. He had known more than one old hard case who said that when the eleven came up, a man was done for. He had known a jugger, a safecracker, one of the best he had ever worked with, who, when the eleven appeared on the back of his neck, was all washed up. Nerve gone, confidence shot, not worth a damn to anybody. If that jugger had been an animal, he would have had the sense to lie down and die.

He looked at his tendons. Maybe he was done for. Maybe he wasn't. Didn't matter. He needed to keep moving. Revenge didn't care what age you were. He'd roll a wheelchair to the ends of the earth to get his revenge, strangle somebody with a colostomy bag if he had to. He promised himself, then and there, whatever happened to his flesh, his will would stay strong. Even as he did, he knew that somewhere, death was laughing at him.

Done with this foolishness, he stepped out of the bathroom and started looking for the cellar stairs. In the old layout there had been stairs going down, but they had been removed. There'd still be some kind of access outside. Maybe the same door he'd used all those years ago.

Then he heard a noise behind him and realized his mistake. Was it the Curse of the Eleven?

He turned and saw the yuppie struggling to stay on his feet in the middle of his own living room. When he saw Hobbs looking at him, the yup said, "Old man, you fucked up now," as if he was trying to sound like a movie. The play was to stay quiet, and not give Hobbs any sign. The yuppie charged low, like a guy who had wrestled in high school, or an idiot.

Hobbs kneed him under the chin. If Hobbs had been whole, the knee would have taken the guy out. But when Hobbs raised his good leg, the bad one gave out. His heel rolled like a hinge full of broken glass and they crashed to the floor together.

The yup had been expecting this even less than Hobbs. He tripped over Hobbs and put his head and part of his arm through the drywall. He fought his way free and dived on Hobbs.

"Fuckyoufuckyoufuckyou," he repeated as if it were some kind of blasphemous mantra. But he wasn't serious about the fucking. He punched ineffectually at Hobbs's ribs in a way that suggested hitting a man in the face was somehow impolite.

Hobbs didn't have this problem. He clawed at the yup's face, trying to catch an eye socket and a lip in the same motion. He got the fishhook and, with a grunt that was more from annoyance than effort, threw the yup off and into the butt end of the sofa.

Hobbs tried to stand, but his ankle wasn't having any of it. He clawed his way up a bookcase, but at an altitude of three feet, the pain was waiting for him. The left side of his body went hot, then numb. All the drive went out of his legs. As he collapsed back to the floor, he managed to grab a terra-cotta statue of the Buddha from a bookshelf. He and the Buddha crashed to the floor together. One of them shattered.

The yup redoubled his attack, this time grabbing Hobbs's neck with both of his dainty hands. The yup squeezed for all he was worth, which wasn't much. In his younger days, Hobbs would have laughed it off. Or maybe taken a nap. Waited for this man to wear himself out with his ineffectual choke. But now, this guy's "not much" was more than enough to do him in. Hobbs heard the roaring in his ears. He saw bright flecks off to the sides of his vision. He tried to roll, but could not.

The yuppie gave a howl that he must have thought was terrifying and barbaric. To Hobbs it sounded like a kitten being strangled. Even as he blacked out, he couldn't believe that this jackass was going to choke him out.

"No," Hobbs croaked.

"Yeah, yeah!" said the yup, who had finally gotten the idea to bang Hobbs's head against the floorboards. "Nobody comes into my house. You understand?" He stopped banging Hobbs's head against the floor so he could ask again, "You understand?"

Holy shit, thought Hobbs, *he wants an answer.* He said nothing, but his right hand scrabbled in the fully and completely awakened shards of the Buddha on the floor next to him. His hand closed on a likely piece just as the yup shrieked, "Huh, who's the man now!"

With what was left of his failing strength, Hobbs jammed the shard of pottery deep into the yuppie's neck. The yup said, "Ow," like he didn't quite understand the whole thing. Then Hobbs pulled the shard toward him, ripping through muscle, tendon, and artery alike. Blood sprayed across the refinished wooden floor. Choking on his fear, the yuppie clamped his hand to his neck, but it was no good. Instead of spurting out sideways, the hot yuppie juice shot up and down.

The yup tried to stand but only stumbled backward three steps. Before Hobbs passed out, the last thing he saw was the man falling backward, bleeding out, into his own bathroom.

EIGHT

Hobbs woke up coughing. There was a raw patch in his throat where the yuppie had tried to choke him. He struggled to his feet and checked the window.

Outside he saw a cop peering in the window of the old truck, his cruiser parked behind it. He saw the cop trigger the radio mic on his vest and say something. Yeah, he'd been made. And here he was in the slaughterhouse, covered in blood. This was bad.

A sharp pain flashed through his head, followed by a wave of exhaustion. He felt that urge that men fighting fires on sinking ships know, that siren song that only men making last stands can hear. *Let it be over. Just lie down and die. Go to your rest and who cares what your "reward" is.* Men who are so hopeless and exhausted that they'd trade in all their tomorrows for a few minutes of peace and an eternity of black silence.

The older you get, the fewer tomorrows you have to trade, and the better the deal begins to look.

He shook it off. With effort he dragged himself into the bedroom. He stripped down, and once again put on somebody else's clothes. These fit a little better. A white button-down shirt and a pair of gray wool pants. The yuppie's shoes were too small for him. He wondered how much longer his socks would hold out.

He found a ball cap with a golf logo on it and slipped it over his head. He used the man's sheet to wipe some of the blood off his face. He thought about going into the bathroom to clean up, but he didn't want to face that idiot's husk.

Mostly he was pissed at himself. It was Hobbs's fault that he had had to kill the yup. If he had done it right at first, none of it would have been necessary. It was sloppy, fucking sloppy.

He checked the front window again. The cop was sitting in his car, typing away on a laptop. *Lucky,* thought Hobbs, *he's waiting for backup. Trusting to the technology.* In the old days that cop would have been knocking on doors and peering through windows. But more cops were on the way. That was the problem with cops. There were always more of them.

Hobbs moved as quickly as he could. Out the back door, down the steps. The backyard was different. Twenty years ago there had been a creek back here. He had crawled along it, dragging a bag of money, as cops swarmed around the mill a mile away and braced his idiot partner, who had scotched the play.

All those years ago, he had slipped into the basement of this house and hid for two days. He got by without food and with what little bit of water he could sneak from the tub of the old-style wringer washing machine tub. When he left, he stole a set of work clothes—little more than rags—and stashed the payroll in a hole he dug in the foundation. He replaced the bricks and hoped for the best. Then he slipped into that stinking little creek—nothing more than a community piss rivulet—and followed it until he came to a train track.

Hobbs had hopped a slow-moving train and was grateful to have gotten out clean.

Money left behind like this was known as a spike, cash you stashed in a place that couldn't be traced to you. They were good to have. Even if you put money in a safe-deposit box, or hotel safe, it was linked to some identity. If that identity got burned, then it wasn't safe to go back. Ever. So, throughout his career, Hobbs had hammered spikes in case he needed them.

Not many of them were left now. He'd never gotten back around to this one. After he had gotten clear of that payroll job, he had hit a good streak and hadn't needed money. When you are rolling in it, you don't want to crawl into a musty basement, or remember the taste of soap flakes in stale water, if you don't have to.

Was it still there? Had it been noticed in the renovations? Maybe some home inspector had quietly pocketed it for himself? There was only one way to know, and he needed to be quick about it.

The door to the cellar had been replaced. The old one hadn't had a lock on it, but this was a proper exterior door with a pattern of nine rectangular glass panes on the top. He rolled up the shirtsleeve around his elbow and gave the pane nearest the knob a pop. It didn't break when he hit it. It popped out of its mounting and landed on the floor. Hobbs reached through and switched the dead bolt.

The floor of the basement was still dirt. That was a good sign. As good a sign as he was going to get on a shitty day like today. And the pane of glass hadn't broken. He was happy to spare his bare feet. He turned on the light and closed the door behind him. There was a whiff of gasoline from a push mower, but underneath it was the same musty scent that haunted him from all those years ago. His lungs hurt as he pushed into the darkness.

This dank space didn't extend the whole length of the house. Twenty-five feet or so in was a block wall. With effort he crawled over that into a crawl space maybe three feet tall. The space was thick with cobwebs and the dried husks of spider crickets. He remembered those things crawling on him in the night, pale and bulbous, nothing like the small, dark, somehow reassuring crickets he had grown up with.

He felt around the base of the retaining wall, feeling for the stone he had placed there long ago. He shuddered a little as he thrust his hand into the darkness. He hadn't been a fearful man. What had changed?

It was still there. Old money in a canvas bank bag, the kind they didn't use anymore. As he pulled on the fabric, he heard it rip and felt the bundles of bills tumble into the dirt. He shoveled the money out with both hands, throwing it over the low wall into the basement space. As he hunched in the dust and mold spores, he felt something land on his neck. He clawed and crushed it and flung it into the darkness with a curse. He bent again and felt that the hole was empty. He took the time to replace the rock.

He gathered the scattered stacks of bills and found it was about $12,000. Not much. Maybe enough. He looked out the window into the backyard. No cops yet. He hadn't heard anybody knocking at the door above, but it was only a matter of time. Sooner or later that knock would come. A cop would waddle around the back of the house, shining his flashlight into the dirty windowpanes. See that one was missing. Hobbs shook off the fear and decided he was going to be a long way away when that happened.

He found an old backpack in some boxes and threw the money into it. Then he took a mountain bike that was hanging off the joists. Ah, yuppies. He scoffed at the helmet at first, but then realized it was perfect. He turned the baseball cap around backward and slid the awkward hunk of plastic onto his head.

He wheeled the bike out and mounted it. The seat didn't have any padding. He felt his balls being separated and crushed, but when he pushed off and started pedaling, it didn't feel so bad. He managed not to fall over. He rode away from the house, deeper into the neighborhood. Ahead of him another cop car turned onto the street and accelerated past him. Hobbs felt his nuts crawl up tighter against the hard bicycle seat, but he reached a hand out and waved to the officer anyway. Just a law-abiding citizen out for a bike ride.

The cop didn't even look at him. He must have been too excited about responding to the APB on the truck. *Just wait till they find that dead yuppie*, thought Hobbs. *That cop's hard-on will probably rip right through his tactical pants.* Hobbs felt a pang of regret for killing the guy. Sure, the yup was probably an asshole, but it was being sloppy that bothered Hobbs.

He shifted. The bike's gears ground and caught and carried him away.

NINE

He pedaled out of the neighborhood slowly, coasting more than anything else. When he was faced with a hill, he had to get off the bike and lean on it, using it to limp his way along the sidewalk.

As he climbed the hill, he passed a mall with a parking lot that looked as if it had been the target of strafing runs by a vengeful Far Eastern air force. The mall was occupied by the conquerors, every sign displaying a name rendered in strange squiggly characters. For a second he thought he could read some of them, but that was from another life, long ago, and he put it from his mind.

He had a sack full of money on his back, and there wasn't a thing he could buy. You might forget an old guy who paid for a pack of gum in cash, but an old guy in socks who buys a pair of shoes and counts out musty bills from an old backpack? You don't forget about that guy. Maybe not ever.

Hobbs pressed on, following the signs back toward the highway. The pain in his leg was worse now, and the exhaustion made his eyes twitch. He didn't know how much farther he could push it, but he wasn't going to stop just because it got hard. That was for the younger, weaker generations—or so he had thought. Until that kid came along.

A wave of emotion almost drove him to his knees. He hadn't thought of Alan since he had woken up. Hadn't thought of any of it, but all of it was driving him anyway. One foot, then another, he pushed the bike to the top of the hill. Before he got there, he found some glass with his foot. The neighborhood was going from "transitional" to crappy.

He cursed and sat on a bench to get the glass out of his foot. The sock soaked up blood. It didn't look too bad, but he had trouble standing on it anyway.

At the top of the hill, he got back onto the bike, nearly falling over, and started down the other side. Part of him, the old, weakened part, wanted to fall asleep with the cool breeze of progress in his face and the droning lullaby of the spokes. He was so busy fighting it off, he rode right past what he needed.

"You lookin' for a good time, baby?" the whore asked, as if she were activated by a motion sensor. Hobbs wasn't looking for a good time, but he stopped anyway. He looked around and spotted what he needed. An extended-stay motel across the street from the tired whore.

Just as every hermit crab needed a shell, every whore needed a flop. That extended-stay would be where she plied her trade. He leaned the bike up against a light pole and limped back to her.

She wasn't that old and she might have been pretty, once. But somebody had beat on her face one too many times. Her eyes were yellow against her chocolate skin, and when she smiled and said, "Hey, baby, you like to party?" she flashed a mouth of ragged teeth, some black, some eaten away up into the gum line, and the rest gone.

"Yeah," Hobbs said, pulling some cash from his pocket, "I like to party."

She looked at his feet and asked, "Somebody steal your shoes?"

He followed her back to the motel. It was four stories tall, with exterior stairways and walkways for room access. She headed toward the stairs.

“Elevator,” Hobbs said, trying to make it sound like a demand, but failing.

“OK, baby. I’ll make it nice and gentle,” the whore said. “What’s your name? I’m Shavonda.”

“Elevator,” said Hobbs.

“I ain’t gonna call you Elevator,” she said, when she pushed the call button.

They rode up in silence. She tried to rub his shoulder, but Hobbs jerked it away and winced in pain.

“OK, OK,” Shavonda muttered.

She was in room 401. The room smelled like cheap air freshener. Below that was the musty funk of old, smoke-soaked carpet and ceiling tiles. There were a king-size bed and an old CRT television. It wasn’t even bolted to the dresser it sat on. Its weight and age were its own security system. It would probably cost more than it was worth to get somebody to carry it downstairs and throw it away.

Shavonda put a hand on her hip and cocked it to one side in an imitation of being sassy. “So what you want? You want me to suck you or fuck you or what? Gon’ cost extra you want any of that kinky shit, and I ain’t gonna shit on you, no way. I gots standards,” she said, laughing at her own words as if she had said something funny. Maybe she had.

Hobbs stepped into the room and looked around. The door to the hallway had caught on a spot where the carpet had bubbled up. Shavonda shuffled past him to close it. She smelled awful. Body odor and a sick chemical reek that she had attempted to cover up with the cheapest of perfumes.

As Hobbs stared at the bed, he heard the door click shut behind him. He asked, “How much for the night? The whole night?”

“Ooh, you real lonely. You just get out of prison, baby?”

Hobbs threw a wad of cash at her and then sat down on the bed. “I need to sleep. There’s more for you in the morning. Even more if you go buy me a pair of shoes—size eleven." Hobbs wrapped his arms through the straps of the backpack and clutched it to his chest. He rolled over on his side and closed his eyes.

"Ooh, baby, don't you worry about me," the old-before-her-time whore cackled, "I be yo' personal shopper."

Hobbs was already asleep.

Much later he was awakened by a tearing sound. He opened his eyes, and saw the tip of a knife in his face.

"You just too old for the street life, you know what I'm sayin'? It ain't my fault. You shouldn't had been up in here in the first place. If it wasn't me, it done would have been somebody else," she said. "I just tryin' to get ahead, same as you."

She moved the knife down between his legs and held it there.

"Now you don't move. See, don't be thinking you gonna change your fate. I'm a old hoochie, and you, you just an old man got robbed. Nothing gonna make you young again. Not one damn thing, you understand?"

Hobbs lay very still.

She flashed her hellish teeth in an imitation of a smile and backed out of the room, brandishing the knife.

Hobbs got up and walked over to the television. The door had gotten caught on the room carpet again, and he could hear the ragged clack of Shavonda's high heels in the distance. He embraced the television. With a grunt he lifted it free from the dresser. There was pain again, but this time it felt good. It felt right. Matched with what he needed to feel and what he needed to do.

He walked out of the room, cables and wires ripping out and trailing free behind him. He walked down the hallway, his feet making no sound in socks. A slight twinge of pain in his foot where the glass had gone in and come out.

He turned the corner and there she was, waiting for an elevator with a stupid look on her battered face.

"What the fuck?" she said, scrambling for her knife. She brandished it and said, "Hell no, cracker, I don't want that television. Go on before you get cut." She pressed the elevator button inanely, as if that would make the car come faster.

Hobbs lifted the television above his head.

"Get the fuck away from me, old man. You got robbed, just deal with it. Call AARP or somebody who gives a fuck," she said as she backed into the stairwell. She kept the knife out in front of her as if it were a talisman, and backed down the stairs, not taking her eyes from him. He stood at the top of the open stairwell holding the old television above his head as if he were a participant in some kind of strange postconsumerist rite.

When she got to the landing, curiosity got the best of her. She looked up at him and had to ask, "What the fuck you gonna do with that television?"

Hobbs did not answer.

Hand on the railing, she edged her way around to the steps, eyes on Hobbs the whole time. She muttered, "My money. Dis *my* money. Stolt it fair and square." When her absurdly high heel rocked over the edge of the step, she caught herself with the railing and looked down.

Hobbs dropped the television.

She looked back up and saw it coming. She started down the stairs and almost got away. The TV caught her on the back of her ankle and she went down, bouncing and tumbling down the flight of stairs in a shower of broken glass and plastic.

Hobbs descended, carefully, one hand on the railing. At his age, he thought with a smile, it paid to be careful.

Shavonda was moaning and trying to clutch her head and the backpack full of money at the same time. It looked as if she thought cash was the antidote to swelling. And why not? It was the antidote to everything else. And the cause of it.

Halfway down the flight, Hobbs stooped to pick up Shavonda's knife. He rose and stepped carefully among the fragments of the shattered television, as if he had all the time in the world.

Through one wild eye, peering out from beneath the bag and the mop of her hair, Shavonda saw him coming. She tried to get up, wobbled uncertainly, and fell. She struggled to rise again.

Hobbs stuck the knife into her leg as if that were where it belonged. She moaned and tried to crawl away. Hobbs pulled the knife out and wiped it on her leg. Her blood looked like hydraulic fluid against her dark, sagging skin.

"Aw fuck, man, you didn't havta do that! Why you do that?"

"Stick to whoring, you're no good at stealing." She let go of the bag without a fight. He didn't stab her again. It was almost civilized.

"You have a car?"

"Fuck you!"

He stabbed her in the leg again. This time she screamed for help. Hobbs hit her in the mouth with the fist that held the knife and managed not to fall over on top of her in the process.

She said, "OK," and spit a little blood out on the concrete. Hobbs looked up and down the stairs. Nothing moved, nobody cared. He had gotten lucky.

"Get up," Hobbs said.

As Shavonda struggled to her feet, she reached out to Hobbs for a hand. When he didn't help, she said, "You ain't nothing but a mean old man. That's all you is. You mean old cracka motherfucker!"

Hobbs was fine with that.

Back in the room, he cut the bedspread into strips. When she saw what was going on, she said, "Aw fuck no. No way." Hobbs shrugged. Then he pressed the knife against her throat smooth and quick. He backed her up to the wall, and when her head touched it, he hit her twice with his elbow. She went out.

He bound her and gagged her and threw her on the bed.

He picked up her bag, a wad of fabric that had once been decorated with sequins; so many of them had fallen off that it now looked as if it had been fashioned from a lizard with a skin disease. He found a foil packet with some powder in it and the keys to a Dodge. Old keys, separate ones for the ignition and the trunk.

He took them and left.

TEN

It looked like a trunk key, but it was worse than a trunk key. It was a hatch key. In the lot, the whore's car stood out as the shittiest turd in the pile. A brown Dodge Omni with the rear bumper hanging half-off. Hobbs thought there was no way the car was going to start. But it turned right over as if the future held hope.

The headliner was falling, and the smell was so bad he rolled down the windows. Didn't matter much, it wasn't as if the air-conditioning worked. He drove until he found an expensive part of town. Big, old houses in a treelined neighborhood. He could smell the money. If he were a small-timer, he would think about knocking one of these off.

It didn't take him long to find what he was looking for. It was a gigantic house in the style of a French château. In the front yard, dwarfed by the expansive lawn and the size of the structure, was a small blue real estate sign—"For Sale."

He turned the next corner until he found what he was looking for. An alley in the back of all the houses. An overgrown remnant from a more civilized time. All these old Southern neighborhoods had them. Remnants of a time when it would have been unseemly to leave your trash in front of your house. When even the milkman knew that it was rude to use the front door when you came to fuck somebody else's wife. All deliveries to the rear.

He drove the car right over the saplings and brush that had grown up in the disused alley. He parked the Omni and got out, leaving the keys in the visor.

He walked the rest of the way to the château. When he peered through the slats in the gate, he couldn't see any sensors or cameras. He used the knife to jimmy the garden latch and let himself into the backyard. Somebody had spent a lot of money letting this yard go in the precise way to make it look like a French country garden. It was a riot of carefully overgrown vines and flowering plants and preweathered antiques.

The sun, bright and hot, the crumbling plaster statues, the scattered wildflowers, all combined to make this yard seem like a ruined corner of some abandoned heaven. Hobbs didn't give it a second look. Heaven wasn't for him.

He headed for the three-car garage on the right side of the house. The door was unlocked. As his eyes adjusted to the cool darkness of the garage, his head spun. The emptiness and the faint smell of oil and gasoline made this room feel like the dead end of something. He put his hand on a wall and closed his eyes until the feeling passed.

The door into the house was locked, knob and dead bolt. Hobbs searched the garage. In an alcove he found garden tools and a potting bench and a rusted old mattock.

He swung the mattock until he'd made a head-size hole in the wall beside the door. Then he reached through and unlocked the door. Before he opened it, he pressed his forehead to its cool surface and took three deep breaths. Hobbs was at the end of himself and he knew it. But he couldn't stop here. If he couldn't defeat the alarm…

He grabbed the knob in his left hand and held the mattock with his right. Then he opened the door and moved as fast as an old man with a limp could manage.

As soon as the door sensor opened, the security system began its urgent and ominous beeping. It led him right to the panel. He smiled at the twenty-year-old hunk of yellowing plastic. Then he hooked the blade of the mattock over the top edge of the panel and raked it off the wall. Bits of drywall rained down on the tile floor, and the panel was left hanging by wires. Hobbs grabbed the wires and gave a yank. They led off to the left.

He threw open a coat closet, empty but for a few boxes, and found what he was looking for. A metal box mounted on the wall. He put the spike of the mattock right through the middle of the door. After a moment's struggle he got the box off the wall. He dropped the mattock, cracking the tile, and took the box under his arm.

The beeping stopped, but Hobbs did not. With the mangled box under his arm, he searched until he found a bathroom. He raked the top off the toilet and dumped the box into the tank. The alarm well and truly defeated, he leaned against the wall and slid down onto the floor.

He sat there, panting, waiting for his heart to slow. He was safe, for now. He resisted the urge to sleep on the tile floor of the bathroom and went in search of a bed.

ELEVEN

"And then the son of a bitch stabbed me in the leg wif my own knife and stole my money! Can you believe that shit?"

"Yes," said Mazerick, trying not to smile. His phone rang.

He answered, saying, "Hang on," and then stepped out of the room. That left Wellsley staring at the foulmouthed, raggedy old whore in her hospital bed.

"You gonna catch that motherfucker or what?" she asked.

"Ma'am, state and federal agencies are working to apprehend him right now," Wellsley said, on autopilot.

"You best better see I get my money back. Stacks and stacks of it. All I done saved during my life of hardship."

Stacks of money, thought Wellsley. Her heart leaped into her throat. But it couldn't be. He couldn't have gotten to it. Must have knocked somebody else off. Maybe that dead guy—but how had he known there would be cash there? That guy in the neighborhood had just been a civilian, a guy who flipped houses for a living.

"Are you even listening to me?"

Wellsley nodded. She let the autopilot drive. "Now this car, was there anything special about it, anything else of value that we should be on the lookout for?"

"That piece of shit never did run right. He ain't gonna get far in it, I promise you that. You let him keep it. Or you take it. I don't give a fuck."

Wellsley became concerned about the call going on in the hallway. She moved to the door and stuck her head out. Mazerick was looking right at her with a curious expression on his face. He jumped a little when he saw her. What did he know?

Of course she hadn't told him the whole truth. What person ever really tells another person the whole truth? But never mind truth, Wellsley was worried about what was being whispered into his ear right now.

Mazerick covered the receiver and said to her, "Found the car." Then he asked the person on the other end of the phone, "And the rest of it?" Wellsley saw his eyes flick toward her and then away. The other thing was definitely about her. He covered the phone and said, "Hey, I gotta handle this, can you finish up with her and then we will roll."

He stepped back out into the hallway without waiting for her agreement. Typical male prick.

Wellsley looked back at Shavonda.

"You ain't got no more questions?" Shavonda demanded.

Wellsley shook her head.

"Well, ain't you gonna go about catching this mans that did this to me? Or don't you care about one more black woman, more or less?"

Wellsley leaned in as close as she could stomach before she said, "Oh, I'm going to get him. But it's your own fault. If you're gonna steal from somebody, you do it right."

Shavonda's mouth hung open. "You ain't sposda do me like that!"

Wellsley said, "Sister, if you act like the weaker sex, you're gonna get treated that way."

In the hallway Mazerick said, "Neighbor called it in. I've got patrol hanging back so we don't spook him. C'mon, Agent, I'm gonna show you the rich part of town."

Rich, thought Wellsley, letting the word reverberate in her brain. *Rich. What really rich person would ever choose to live in this landlocked town?*

As he drove them to the scene, Mazerick let it fly. "I checked with a buddy of mine in the *bureau*."

Wellsley kept her eyes on the scenery sliding by as she said, "Yeah."

"Yeah," said Mazerick. It was an old cop trick. Never ask until you know the facts. The facts aren't what you want when you question somebody. What you want is the emotion, the reaction to the facts. Anybody can fake a fact. Almost nobody can fake an emotion. They can hide it or suppress it, but not fake it. So she just sighed, stared out the window, and waited.

Mazerick broke first. "You want to tell me?"

"You say it."

"You've been suspended, removed from duty pending investigation. Why didn't you tell me that?"

She tried to get tears to come, but they wouldn't. Maybe she hated this guy too much. Maybe she just wasn't weak enough to cry anymore. So she turned and told the truth, eyes not wavering from Mazerick.

"I needed your help. And I thought, if I told you the truth, you wouldn't help me."

"Did you kill your partner?"

Wellsley got hot. "Yeah, I shot him dead. That's why I've come all this way to catch this bastard whose name I don't even know. It's not like this jackass killed my partner Barry and ruined my career. No, that's not what's driving me at all," she said, dripping with sarcasm.

"Easy, easy," said Mazerick, taking one hand off the wheel in a gesture of surrender. "Hold your fire. I'm not out to get you. I just like to know what I'm getting into. Especially when a pretty face tends to cloud my decision making."

She looked back out the window to hide her eye roll. Fucking pig. The ugly side of the damsel in distress. It was all just a cover for taking advantage of a woman in a vulnerable situation. That old fairy tale was just a good-looking duvet on a thick comforter filled with centuries of rape.

"You seem like good people," he said, and put a hand on her knee. It was the kind of gesture a father might make, or an uncle. *Yeah*, thought Wellsley, *an uncle, the kind that likes to touch little girls when nobody else is around.* She was proud of herself for not screaming. "I don't think any of my partners would have done this for me. Be lucky if any of those pricks showed up at my funeral. And if they did, it'd just be to bang my wife. So if they ask me, I don't know nothing."

She choked out the word, "Thanks."

When they found the car it barely qualified as hidden. As they drove by they could see the back of the ancient Dodge from the street. Mazerick pulled a U-turn and eased up next to the patrol car.

"Haven't seen anything since we spotted it," said the cop.

"Thanks," said Mazerick. And to Wellsley, "You want to take a look?"

"Ladies first," said Wellsley.

Mazerick grinned.

As they approached the alley, Mazerick asked, "You got a piece?"

"No," she lied.

Mazerick stepped behind the fence and knelt. He pulled a wheel gun from his ankle holster. A hammerless, blued .38. He handed it to her low, where the patrol cop couldn't see, saying, "It was my grandfather's. It's good luck."

No, it's not, she thought.

"If you shoot somebody with it, we'll figure out a story," he said, and winked with a leer.

She instantly thought of a story in which the man got a hold of Mazerick's backup piece and killed him with it. She ran it several ways quick in her head. Would it be better for the story if she said she got Mazerick's gun and killed the old man? Or would it be better if she said Mazerick got the shot off? It would depend on the scene, but it would be better if he got the shot off. The last act of a hero cop, killing the guy who'd shot him and saving her. Because, of course, she didn't have a weapon. She was on suspension. Yeah. That would be better. Make that damsel-in-distress shit work for you.

They each took a side of the overgrown dirt alley between the mansions. Guns out, stepping carefully, they advanced toward the car. Mazerick moved smoothly and cautiously. He wasn't great, thought Wellsley, but he was good, and, in contrast to his big mouth, he was careful.

The windows were rolled down. From opposite sides of the car they peeked in, guns first. Trash, and a terrible smell. On the backseat Wellsley saw an empty condom box.

She pointed to it with the tip of her weapon and said, "Classy."

Mazerick said, "Full service."

Jesus, thought Wellsley. "So where'd he go?"

Mazerick looked around. "He holed up somewhere."

"Stole another car?"

"Has to be tired. He's an old man, and wounded," said Mazerick.

They walked around to the back of the car. As Mazerick peered through the dirty glass of the hatchback, Wellsley asked, "You wanna go a little further?"

Mazerick frowned.

She could see that he wanted to call for backup. That would fuck everything up. So Wellsley leaned in and kissed him hard. To keep the bile down, she thought about killing him. When she let him up for air, he was flushed and had a stupid look on his face. She could see that all the blood had rushed from one head to another, so she said, “He’s an old man. Let’s just go get him.”

Mazerick smiled and nodded as if he were John Wayne. He was a dumbass, thought Wellsley. Just the dumbass she needed.

TWELVE

Hobbs had crawled into the master bed and drawn the comforter around him like an animal. There were no sheets, but he was too tired to care.

When he awoke, he didn't open his eyes. He had slept so deeply that he couldn't feel his body. His thoughts drifted between waking and sleeping. Where was he? What did he have to do? And why?

As it came back to him in pieces, he had less and less desire to open his eyes. He wanted to sleep. To sleep forever. But he knew that the growling in his stomach and the pressure on his bladder would force him to move sooner than he wanted.

How had it started? And now that it had started, how would it end? He thought of Grace, and her golden hair in the wind, and the light off the lake. He thought of the wonder of having found her. He had told himself that he needed nothing and no one, so many times that he had almost believed it.

For an instant he thought of seeing if there was a phone in this shell of a house. But he could not call her. He did not exist. And he could not be linked to Grace. Maybe a pay phone? To hear her voice again. To feel her soft touch and her silly whispers as they lay in bed in the early morning. He had always thought that these desires were weakness. But now he drew strength from them.

He couldn't call. He couldn't go back. Not until it was done, one way or the other. And not until he was clear of it. When he got that money, what would Grace want to do? Could she even launder all of it?

He knew without having to ask her, as he knew the rhythm of her breathing while she slept and the spaces between her heartbeats as she lay still after they had made love. She wanted nothing else but the simple lake house and a life with him. But why was that not enough for him? Why was it that whenever he was with her, he wanted to be away? And whenever he was away, he wanted to be there?

He had been a fool not to be content with what he had. A more philosophical man would have seen a kind of justice in his predicament. Hobbs missed the irony, but recognized that he had taken a job he didn't need for more money than he could ever use. He just couldn't stop working. He was too old to do anything else. He had always believed that he was an old soldier who would die in the harness, come wind, come wrack. But now, during this pause in the action, he wondered if he could truly escape.

If he could walk away, sidestep all of it. He recognized these thoughts as symptoms of weakness and fatigue, but he did want to talk to Grace. To tell her those things he never had. To tell her he was sorry that he was the way he was. That he was undeserving of her. And that all he wanted to do was come home.

But he would not be able to promise that when it was done, he would stay. That he would never work again. The call itself would only increase the chance of her being in danger. A stupid risk. By now she probably thought he was dead. What had it been—three months? Four? Theirs was a relationship out of time, as if from the days of sailing ships, one of long separations and happy reunions.

He had to see it through to the end. For Hobbs there was no way out but through. Then he remembered how it had started. He had been shooting squirrels.

He heard a noise from downstairs and opened his eyes.

PART TWO
TAKING UP THE GUN

ONE

Three months before

The drugs were late this week. Alan knew, because he kept track. He quantified just about everything. How long he slept, how many steps he took, when the guy brought his mother's drugs. But he didn't need a calendar to keep track of that. When she ran out, she'd get all shrieky and angry. And she was running out earlier and earlier each week. Even at twenty-two Alan knew not to try telling her that. He knew what she was. And so did she.

When all the pills were gone, she'd start calling Uncle Tommats. First she'd yell at him. "Where is that dirty spic with my medicine? I think he ran off with it. Send somebody else."

If the "medicine" still didn't come, she'd start feeling so bad she'd beg. "C'mon, Tommy. You know I don't have anybody to take care of me now that my *husband* is away." She'd never call Alan's dad by his name. Always "my husband." And she'd never say "prison" or "jail." It was always "away."

She'd never say what Tommats was. A gangster, not exactly like in the movies, but close enough, and her lover. But everybody knew. Everybody knew what everybody else was, except Alan. Nobody knew what he was. Not even Alan.

Mostly he kept his head in his laptop. Except when one of his quantifiable alarms went off. Then he would get up and do the perfect number of exercises for his fitness level. He was doing push-ups when the drugs came.

At the front door of the apartment, his mother snatched the brown paper bag and slammed the door without saying a word. She scurried through the living room and slammed the door to her bedroom. Thank God. Having her passed out would make it easier to focus on what he had to do.

Alan racked off another ten push-ups, then returned to the couch. He hooked a pair of closed headphones over his ears, opened his laptop, and disappeared from the real world. Not for the first time, he thought, *The real world sucks.* But when he quantified that statement, he had to admit he hadn't seen much of it.

The theme music of a massively multiplayer online role-playing game called the Universe of Strife filled his ears. The only sound in the apartment was the gentle scratching of gaming mouse against cushion, and the muted clicks of the W, A, S, and D keys as he tapped them to move his character through the game.

In this other universe, he and everybody else knew who he was. A level-seventy dark elf assassin named Romagos. He was powerful. He was respected. He was feared.

In the game he was traversing a range of purple iridescent mountains on a griffin that streamed fire from its wings. As his steed crested the mountains, Alan joined his guild channel. Immediately the voices of friends and allies poured into his ears. "Romagos!" they cried. "Romagos is in this with us, now we are sure to win." He landed in the middle of a massive guild battle against the Red Swords of Tyndalos Guild.

The plan was that Romagos would envelop himself in concealment, sneak around behind the skirmish line, and bring down as many of the enemy as he could. He would start with the healers, which in turn would make it easier to bring down the frontline fighters, known as tanks.

When the barrier dropped and the match started, Alan pressed F2 and his character turned invisible.

Then he hit the backtick key and typed a very special command. A world away—he knew not where—his request was answered in the affirmative.

His invisible sash changed colors from blue to red and put the Knife of Night to work on his former guild. He tore through the back ranks in under a minute. By the time his stealth effect timed out, the Swords of Tyndalos had won. Alan didn't concern himself with the mopping up. He logged out of the game and opened a web browser. When he checked his account balance, there it was! Thirty thousand dollars in cold digital currency. Alan giggled. This was an act of treachery that would live forever. Nobody had ever done it before, and he was sure that both the game developers and the players would work hard to make sure that no one could ever do it again. He had changed the game forever.

But most important to Alan was that he had planned, plotted, and executed a perfect crime. It wasn't against any laws in the real world, but he had broken laws and customs and trusts—the norms of reasonable behavior—and been well paid for it. He closed his laptop and got up.

The urge to play the game, which had once been all-consuming, was now gone and would never return.

Thirty thousands of dollars. He could understand, but he couldn't believe it. He knew what the game had meant to him and what it meant to other people, but that the Red Swords would take up a collection, and pay that much for dominance in a game, a *game* that wasn't in any way real...

Because that's what this crime had done for him. It had made it real. Alan didn't need money. Nobody needed money with Uncle Tommats around. But Uncle Tommats's gifts always came with strings and control. He liked his uncle, even though he was pretty sure his uncle had gotten his dad sent to prison so he could rail his mom. From what he knew of his dad, Alan was pretty sure he was better off with his uncle. But Alan would never be his own man trapped under Tommats's wing.

He wanted a place in the world. A challenge, an identity. Mom wanted him to go to college. Uncle Tommats wanted him to go to college. But Alan thought that was for suckers. He wanted to be a criminal, not like his dad, but like his uncle. He hadn't gone to college. And he was rollin' in cash. He didn't put up with shit from anybody.

Why not? He watched the news. They were all criminals. Everybody successful was shady about something. And everybody knew it. Playing it straight and working hard was for suckers. So was trust. Nah, man, he wasn't gonna be a gangster, or a mobster. He wanted to be an organized, quantified criminal. For real. Besides, he was smart. Smart people really shouldn't have to work hard.

He got up and snagged a Diet Coke from the fridge. He tried watching TV, but his attention span didn't let him lock on to anything.

TWO

When the fan on his laptop stopped, Alan opened it again. His chat program was going nuts. Questions, death threats, people wanting to know what the hell had happened. He killed the window and the program. In an instant, all that bored him. He had been a somebody, but not in the real world. He had pulled a job, but not in the real world. He needed…

He didn't know what he needed, but he needed something more.

Out of boredom he started digging through a dump of files from a JPMorgan Chase breach. This was old, dead data. There were so many credit card numbers available online, individual numbers now went for less than a dollar. But those weren't all that was in here. Those were just all that everybody he knew online was interested in.

He paged and paged and paged, looking for—anything, nothing, everything, something. It was hopelessly boring accounting data. There was probably something cooked about these numbers, but it was a con that the bankers had already run. It seemed there was nothing to hack.

Then Alan had an idea. Instead of looking for something that looked good to him—a bored, tech-savvy kid with a computer, just like a million other bored, tech-savvy kids with computers—Alan decided to seek out the most boring, useless piece of data in the entire archive.

Bank branch reconciliation statements were pretty boring, but they did show where the cash was and how it moved. The kind of data that a bank robber might use if those idiots were smart enough to do anything other than rob a bank. But nobody except Alan had much time for it. Why? It was so much easier to steal on the data layer.

After invoking strange words of command-line power—*sed, grep, awk*—on those files, he decided that data wasn't useless enough. He copied it all off in a directory for later, and kept looking.

He found a bunch of files—huge files—all with broken headers, all out of sequence. After some fiddling he put them back together. They were a record of federal and state benefit payments. A little Googling revealed that JPMorgan Chase processed EBT and disability payments for the federal government and most of the states. JPMorgan Chase took a cut of every penny provided through a range of programs that had once been known as food stamps.

Alan shook his head and whistled in admiration. This was a skim. A real game. Made guys like his uncle look so small they disappeared. And his dad? Well, his dad had always looked like an idiot to Alan. That's why he'd wound up in jail.

He found a line that read, "Physical transfers." It was all listed by state and route and date. There were transfers and amounts and location addresses. It was a massive amount of data, impossible to make sense of just by paging through.

He opened a text file and in the first line he typed, "import gmaps." Twenty minutes and seventeen syntax errors later, a map of the United States showed transfers pulsing in real time as the time scale at the bottom traveled through the last year. He set it on loop and stared at it for a while, letting his mind blank out.

As he watched he wondered if this nonexpectant blankness was what the drugs were like for his mom. Probably not, he thought. She just slept, numb to the world. The anger came from deep within, but he pushed it aside. Feeling sorry for himself. He could have had it a lot worse. She could have abused him. He never considered that being ignored was abuse, and maybe worse than being hit. Maybe worse than being burned with cigarettes.

Then he saw it. It was the kind of thing you could easily miss. Every other week, a fat pulse across the top of Florida. A very fat line. It was so big he thought it was a glitch, some bad characters in the source file, but it wasn't. It was a shitload of cash on a truck. He zoomed in on the area and watched the money flow.

He had just made $30,000 by being smart. But it was chump change. By being smart and having some balls, he could really pull one over. Take everything he could ever need and then some. He'd be done. Fuck the whole crazy, full-of-shit world. Fuck Mom. Fuck Dad. Fuck Tommats. He'd have his.

It was exactly the kind of thing that kids who sat behind computers could never pull off. Leave the house? Nah, there's not even air-conditioning out there. Talk to other people? Scary.

Even as he made fun of them he recognized that he was one of them. He felt the shivers run from his neck down to his fingertips. He couldn't pull this off. No way. Not alone. But there were guys. Pros. Guys with untraceable guns. Guys who knew how to open an armored car. Guys with money to finance. He had $30,000. That had to be a start, right? But he had the feeling that $30,000 wouldn't be enough.

He thought he would sell the job. But after pulling up a web browser and masturbating furiously to Japanese porn, he realized he didn't really want to sell the job. Just as he didn't really want to make love to a girl on a screen. He wanted the real girl. He wanted the real money. He wanted the real action.

He wanted a real life.

THREE

He could smell her and hear her breathing, but he couldn't see her from the doorway. The room was dark, and it smelled as if she had pissed the bed. Wouldn't be the first time that had happened. He didn't even like coming in here. He loved his mom, as all boys do, but she loved pills more than she loved him—than she loved anything.

He waited on the threshold for a few minutes, waiting to hear her breathing change, or for her to roll over in bed. When she didn't, he sighed. It would be easier to say fuck you than goodbye. This way he could just get what he'd come for and leave.

It was in the closet.

Even Alan knew that the closet was a stupid place to hide something valuable. It was the first place a smart thief would look. But people hid things there anyway. His mom had probably forgotten she had put it there.

He walked through the bathroom and stepped onto the thick pile carpet of the walk-in closet. He pulled the door shut before he turned on the lights. On either side, all the way back, were dresses. Tommats had bought them for Alan's mother. They were beautiful, but she never wore them anymore. She never did much of anything, except swallow pills and go to sleep.

Uncle Tommats used to come around to visit. Checkin' up on his nephew, he would say. But then he would take his nephew's mother into the bedroom. Alan knew what was going on. One of those times, Tommats had been drunk. And he'd left it behind.

Alan found it in a shoebox in the far back corner of the closet, under a pile of hangers.

It was heavy and black and ugly. It had a snub nose and a huge cylinder. The bullets were so big there were only five of them. He cocked the hammer back with his thumb. Then he worked the pistol with both hands, pulling the trigger and letting the hammer down slowly. The force with which that hammer wanted to snap back into place scared him. The hammer felt eager, hungry. What if he let it slip?

He put the pistol into his waistband as he had seen people do in the movies and on TV. Before he could even get out of the closet, it fell out on the carpet, landing with a muffled thud. He put it in his pocket, shut off the light, and opened the door.

Alan was certain that he hadn't made a sound. But as he crossed the bedroom, his mother moaned and tossed in the bed. He saw her open her bloodshot eyes. She blinked hard and opened her eyes wide, struggling to see. It was her, thought Alan. It was his mom. She was going to ask him what he was doing. She was going to tell him not to go, because she loved him.

But when she spoke, she asked, "Tommy, is that you? Did you bring the pills?"

Alan left without answering.

FOUR

The next day Alan went to visit his dad. It was just as it had always been. A plexiglass window between them. An ancient Bakelite phone on a metal cord to connect them. Some kids played catch. Alan talked to his dad on the prison phone.

"Lookie there, I must be somebody special. Everybody wants to see me today. I thought you were my lawyer," said his dad, disappointed to see him.

"Jimmy, I'm looking for a guy," said Alan.

"I'm sorry to hear that, *Son*, although that would make you very popular in here."

"Fuck you, *Dad*. You want to help me or not? Based on our track record, I'd go with no, but I thought I might give you a chance to get a few checks out of the shitheel column."

"Is that any way to greet your father?"

"You want me to hug this plexiglass? Kiss the phone? You know the deal, old man."

Jimmy, his dodge and bravado spent, slumped in weariness and looked like the caged animal he was. He asked, "OK, flash, what the fuck can I do for you in here?"

"I got a job of work. And I need a very specialized contractor."

A look of disappointment and sadness crossed the older man's face. "No, Al, you don't want to go into that line."

"Oh, really, Jimmy? What would your advice be? Plastics? Maybe I should sell tires? Those things sure worked out for you."

"I made mistakes."

"Yeah, you did."

"Son…I…"

"Stop with that bullshit. That *son* bullshit. You know what a father does? A father is there. You, you were never there." Alan paused, held the phone away from his mouth, and wrestled with his emotions. He hated to show weakness in front of his father.

On the other side of the thick plastic, marred by the scratches and deformed by the curve in the material, Jimmy waited.

"I was trying to be cool about this," continued Alan, after a time, "but that's not working. Are you gonna help me or not?"

Jimmy sighed and asked, "You're gonna do this anyway?"

"I need a guy to put it together and run it. I'll probably just sell the whole thing to him. But it's big. It needs the best. Just gimme a name. A phone number. I'll cut you in."

Jimmy shook his head violently. "I don't want a cut. Not from you. And it doesn't work that way."

"What? The guy doesn't have a name? Doesn't have a phone number?"

"No," he said. Then he told his son how it worked. That is, if enough people who had been involved were still alive and working. "The guy you want was called Hobbs."

"Is he dead?"

"Or in prison. But if he's not, he probably doesn't use the same name anymore."

"What?"

"When you take things, people get angry."

"Right, so how do I find him?"

"You go to a bar in Philly. You ask for him. If they think you're right, they'll get in contact with him."

"Jesus Christ," said Alan, "You been in here for a while. You know there's this thing called e-mail, right? You know about e-mail?"

"They can't catch a guy they can't find a trace of."

"Was that your mistake?" Alan asked.

Jimmy looked away and said, quietly, "I made a lotta mistakes."

"How about you make up for one or two of them by giving me the name of that bar."

"Call me Dad," said Jimmy.

"You gotta be fucking kidding me with that shit," said Alan.

"I'm sorry, Alan."

"Well, that's nice for you, what's the name of the bar?"

"You say it."

"What do you want?" asked Alan.

"I want to hear you say it."

"No, what do you really want? You want a house in the country, with a white picket fence? Slippers and pipe? You want to be Dad, is that it?"

Feeling foolish, Jimmy nodded.

"Well, it ain't gonna happen. You fucked it up. And nothing I can do can make it right."

"We could try," said Jimmy, "I mean, I don't know how to do it, but we could try. Would you want to try? Would you, Al?"

"Sure, you could push me on the swing and throw the ball around and we'd go get ice cream," said Alan, sticking the knife in and feeling around for Jimmy's liver.

"Hey, I'm tryin' here."

"Sorry, old man, (a) you're never getting out of this hole and (b) I ain't got time for this father-son reunion bullshit."

"I'm sorry. I'm tryin' to better myself. I just don't know how to do it. I know, I know…"

"I'll tell you what I know, *Jimmy*. I'm pretty sure blackmailing your kid into calling you Dad isn't a good start."

Jimmy was quiet a long while. When he accepted defeat, he said, "Smeagles."

"Sméagols?"

"Yeah, Smeagles," Jimmy said.

"Thank you." Alan hung up the phone. His dad sat there and watched his son leave, staring at the wavy plexiglass until the guard told him it was time to go.

FIVE

Grace sat in the breakfast nook and watched him through the bay window. There was movement in the tree, but he remained perfectly still, waiting for the perfect shot. Patience was, when she reflected upon it, the reason he had been such a good thief. The ability to hold his nerve in check.

Why couldn't he retire? Recognize that the best of the game was up? Not that his nerve was shot, or his will had weakened. He was just old. Everybody loses a step. Why couldn't he see that?

When she had asked him about it, he had growled at her. But every time he came back from a job he would shake his head and say, "That's it. I'm off it. Too many cameras. Too many amateurs. The take's always too small."

It had been nearly six months since the last one. And he had grown grumpier and grumpier, more and more insufferable as the machinery inside him ground away at him. This morning he hadn't even sat down to breakfast. He'd gotten a .22 rifle from the garage and set up on the tree.

He watched the tree with patience, so she watched him with patience and hope. Was this it? The turning of the wheel? The moment when he would finally come home to her to stay?

If not this moment, it would come. It would *have* to. And soon, she thought. The wisdom in her old bones whispered to her, "At this age, honey, change only goes in one direction."

Through the window she watched Hobbs, the man who was and was not her husband. Of course he had not married her.

There had been no ring, no exchange of vows, no signatures on marriage licenses. What name would a man without firm identification use? But all the same, she was his and he was hers, as surely as one person could be another's. And so it had been for nearly thirty years now.

He, of course, denied this fact. All men who imagine themselves red-blooded deny their domesticity. Why, just look at him, sitting in a lawn chair with that rifle laid across his lap. He stared intently at the bird feeder hanging amid the branches of the willow tree. He was waiting for squirrels—damn thieves, he called them. Why he cared at all about the squirrels, Grace could never know. They had plenty of bird food and money enough not only for all their needs, but to feed all the squirrels around this entire lake.

If nothing else, Grace thought, he should have professional courtesy toward the squirrels. Perhaps it was the pettiness, she thought. Perhaps he would have been more tolerant if he had caught the squirrels in the act of breaking into the garage and dragging a twenty-five-pound bag of seed away. Or, even more impossibly, trying to drive away with it in the pickup. A seed at a time had never been Hobbs's style. Small jobs were beneath him. He was a thief, but anything but petty.

When he had spoken to her of his work (which was almost never) he'd referred to himself and his now-dwindling band of associates as "heavy heisters." Men who used courage and daring to steal large sums all at once. Men who were good behind the wheel and steady on the trigger. Hobbs provided the planning and the whip hand. She had seen him work only once, that first time.

She had been on the grift in those days. She was on the arm of a precious metals dealer whom she had convinced to betray his partners. With her prodding he had fingered the job, and a second man, Bill Presque, had brought Hobbs in to run it. She'd thought she had a taste for it—the danger, the rough games of take and double cross—but when that job had gone wrong, when her grift was lying on the floor at her feet trying to stop up the bullet holes in his chest with his fat fingers, she realized she wasn't who she had thought she was.

For years she had not been able to think about it. Let alone speak of it. But after they had bought the house on the lake, the passage of time, quiet seasons, had caused the horror of those days to fade. Hobbs had rescued her from that. And she had rescued him, or was trying. She had knit a careful, patient net around him, one he couldn't see and didn't realize he was struggling against.

With patience she watched him from the windows. Waiting for his restlessness to fade away. Waiting for her man to come home to her for good.

With a fluid motion he brought the rifle to his shoulder and fired. Down by the water a squirrel fell dead from the willow tree.

She watched him get up and go to the boathouse. He came back out with a sack, filled it with the squirrels, and threw them off the end of the dock.

She jumped when the kitchen phone rang. The metal hammer vibrating between metal bells was an angry noise. She looked at it without getting up. It rang again. It was ugly on the wall. The only thing in the kitchen that was still harvest gold. She did not want to answer it. She knew what it would be.

She said hello, listened, hung up the phone, and went to Hobbs.

SIX

Hobbs had sat there and killed seven of those damned tree rats, and it hadn't made him feel a bit better about anything. Stupid, stupid squirrels. Blindsided by an obvious trap. After the first couple, they should have gotten wise to the game. Didn't they see the pile of bodies beneath the tree? They had to see them. They just weren't smart enough to stay away. Hunger got the best of them. Dead for birdseed they didn't even need. They just wanted it.

Sick of killing squirrels, he got up and hooked the .22 under his arm. In the boathouse he found an old sack. He filled the bottom with fist-size stones from the riprap. His hands looked like weathered claws seeking among the rocks.

He gathered the squirrel corpses in the sack and tied the top in a knot. Then he threw them off the end of the dock and watched them sink where he liked to drop a line. Little thieves could bring the catfish. Maybe later he'd catch the catfish. If he lasted that long.

He looked up toward the house. A fixed address, by God. He'd never thought he'd have that. That was Grace's doing. She had wanted the house, said they needed it for a write-off. She was a good woman, but she hadn't been when he'd met her. Beautiful, sure, but salty, and working her ass for all it was worth. He'd been through a string just like her. And even now, nearly thirty years later, he couldn't figure out what was different about her.

He'd taken her from a weak-chinned finger who was already betraying his partners. He'd never fooled around on the job much, but the man's lack of loyalty offended him. And, well, the obvious, low cleavage and long legs that she paraded around in front of him like it was on sale, made it easy to make an exception. Now, even at fifty, she was hot enough to melt the ice on the front walk. That joke had made her smile for the last fifteen years.

The lake house was the perfect backdrop for that joke. In the beginning they had come here only during the winter months, when the lake was abandoned. The rest of the time they'd lived in hotels and on room service. Once or twice a year, he'd pull a job. But here, Grace said, they could be themselves. And perhaps they were. Sometimes Hobbs had trouble remembering what his real name was, especially up here in the snow. And his *self*? He honestly had no idea.

He was the job. And when he wasn't on the job, he was antsy. As he was now. He didn't know how much longer he could hang around here. Nothing had come together in a while. Everything seemed harder now. As if the world had changed. But maybe he was just older.

Once Grace had teased him about retiring. It had started harmlessly enough. She was stroking her fingers through his closely cropped gray hair. She told him how the years looked good on him. And that this gray was a sign that it was time for Hobbs to retire so they could grow old together.

He had stiffened and turned, gotten up from in front of the fireplace, and fixed himself a drink. She had followed, missing the signal, still teasing. Telling the old man to pack it in. The times were moving too fast for him. It was one of the only times he had hit her, and he had immediately regretted it.

She had turned away and held her hand to her face for a long time. Then she had turned back, looking at the blood from her lip. She had reached down with her bloody hand and grabbed a few cubes of ice. She'd brought them to her lips, trying to be tough girl about it, but Hobbs could see the tears in her eyes.

He had shaken his head and almost apologized. She had thrown the ice in his face and kissed him, warm and salty and tasting of blood. They'd made love, right there, as they had the first time—when they had cheated death and the law and had made it out alive. When they were done, that's when Hobbs had realized there was something wrong with him. A hole in the water of his soul that he just couldn't fill.

They had gotten away with it. She once. He many times. They had escaped death and betrayal and jail. This was supposed to be *it*. This life with this beautiful woman, not rich, but beyond the cares of money, this was the prize. How many had he seen go down to the grave or up to the pen? And as they breathed their last or as the cellblock clanged shut behind them, this—this very moment that Hobbs had—wasn't this what they had prayed for?

For Hobbs, it was not enough.

He rubbed his eyes. In the darkness behind his lids he saw the glassy-eyed squirrels in a pile below the tree, saw them disappearing into the sack. Saw the sack sinking into the blackness of the lake water.

From the house he heard the phone ring. Not a shitty electronic warble, but the honest sound that was made when one piece of metal slammed into another, bell-shaped piece of metal.

Grace waved him up to the house. The bell tolled for him.

As he walked to the house, he thought maybe the thing that drove him was the same thing that caused the squirrels to climb over a pile of dead bodies for a chance at the feeder.

In the kitchen he picked up the phone and said, "Hobbs."

On the other end of the line was a gruff voice, the kind that sounded as if it ate cigars for lunch. The voice said, "I'm closing the place down. If you want to pay ya tab or ya respects, come ahead. If you don't, then the hell wit' cha." Then the voice hung up.

"Who was it?" asked Grace.

Hobbs replaced the phone on its hanger and said, "I gotta go see a guy."

"When?" she asked.

"Tomorrow."

"But it's your birthday!" she said.

Hobbs went back outside.

SEVEN

Smeagles had been an old-fashioned kind of neighborhood bar in an old-fashioned kind of neighborhood. It was the kind of dive you could depend on. One that would lend money, store luggage, and, most importantly for Hobbs, take messages. It was owned and operated by Sean Cleary, a former associate of Hobbs's who had decided that for his "retirement" he would open a sports bar.

Cleary had gotten the money to buy the joint from working a bank job with Hobbs back in the salad days. They had knocked off the Farmers and Merchants Bank of Altoona by firing a stolen howitzer through the lock mechanism. They hadn't wasted time on that job, they'd backed a dump truck right through the brick wall and fired the gun right from the bed.

They were in and out in under ten minutes. A noisy ten minutes, but then that was back when noisy was OK. No way in hell anybody could pull that job today. Too many cameras. Too many cell phones, sensors, and radios. The cops would come on like a hammer. Hell, cops didn't even look like cops anymore. They all dressed as if they were going to invade the Middle East after lunch. Acted like it too.

When Cleary bought the bar, the guys he worked with regular-like were certain he would be back on the job inside a year. How long could it take to drink the inventory? What a storybook mistake. Literally the start of a joke. So this Irishman buys a bar...

But he hadn't. To start with, he was too broke. Too broke to even buy a sign. So he had borrowed a brush and painted "Smear 'Em, Eagles!" on a piece of stolen plywood. He propped his "sign" next to the door. That's all it took. Joint was packed from then on in. As time passed and the sign faded, the name was shortened. When Cleary sprang for a new sign, the place was Smeagles and that was it.

The neighborhood around it was a hell of a lot nicer than it had been when he opened. Old buildings had turned to condos, new condos had been put up. And Smeagles had thrived. As Hobbs circled the block looking for a parking space, he felt a small twinge of gratitude for that. Times may change, he thought, but Smeagles would remain.

As he pushed into the darkness of the bar, the smell was familiar. A place where life's frustrations were vented on the liver. But something was wrong. It was bright. As bright as he had ever seen it. There were fluorescent lights on the ceiling. They looked as if they had been there since light was invented, but Hobbs had never seen them turned on before.

"We're closed for renovations," said a young man in a tie. He didn't look up from his sheaf of plans laid out on a table.

Hobbs didn't even break stride.

"I said…," said the man, but trailed off when Hobbs stepped uncomfortably close to him. The younger man took a step back.

"What's this?" Hobbs asked.

"I…I…said," said the young man in the tie.

"What's your name?"

"Michael, who—"

"Where's Cleary?"

From the back room Hobbs heard Cleary's voice say, "Let that man alone, Son. He's here to pay his tab!"

Cleary waddled out of the back, hitching up his pants up around his gut.

"Mikey, this here is one of my oldest surviving associates, Mr.—" He paused to let Hobbs fill in the rest.

"Caspar. Caspar, Ronald Caspar from Denver."

"Yes, lad, Ronnie and me go way back."

"Just not by that name?" Michael asked. He looked back and forth between his father and Hobbs. Then he shook his head. "I don't want to know."

"No," said Hobbs, "you don't. Cleary, what the fuck is this?"

"Progress, Mr. Caspar, pro-gress," said Cleary with a smile that looked as if it had been used as a getaway car.

"I just need you to sign this, Dad, and I'm on my way," said Michael.

Hobbs poured himself a short beer and took a seat at the bar while father and son tended to their business. When they were done, Mikey shut off the overhead lights. Cleary came over and sat on the bar stool next to him.

"He's takin' over the place," Cleary said without being prompted.

"You couldn't have told me that over the phone?"

Cleary looked hurt. "Why, I thought you'd want to come by and pay your last respects to the place, such as it was. 'Fraid it'd be too much of a strain on your auld heart if you came by and the place had been all yuppified wi'out me warning you."

Hobbs sipped his beer.

"I'm not detecting the proper note of gratitude for my enduring and undying friendship," Cleary said, reaching over to clink his glass against Hobbs's. "You know, it's not yer fault yer bitter, Hobbsy, it all wen' to shit when they shot Kennedy."

Hobbs shook his head and made a noise in the back of his throat.

"Nah, you think about it. You're slowin' down now, or will be soon enough. You'll see. You'll have plenty of time to think. It's time, Hobbs, it's time. Time to shed the auld life like a tree weepin' leaves in the fall. Time to step down and give the young ones a chance. I mean, can you believe it? The set of coincidences that had to occur for me to wind up with a boy like Michael. And then not to fuck him up so bad that he couldn't get into college. And then have the kid actually graduate from college—work hard and get a loan to buy his old man out. Who would loan the likes of us money?"

"Nobody ever needed to," Hobbs said.

"Ah, but listen to me, gettin' all maudlin and weepin' like the old Irish bastard I am." He raised his glass. "No reason for me to be cryin'. I'm just about to start my second retirement. A lotta guys don't even live to see one."

"Some guys don't even want one," Hobbs said, quietly, into his beer.

"Don't say that, Hobbs. Or Caspar or whatever you're callin' yourself these days for the purposes of trade. You put your feet up and enjoy your dotage."

Hobbs sucked down the rest of his beer and planted the glass on the bar. "I'll quit when I'm done. Last time I checked we were square. You call me here because you ran out of friends?"

"Someone asked for you."

"Who?"

"Young fella, fulla sand."

"Young fella? Heat?"

"I don't think so."

Cleary walked behind the bar and punched NO SALE on the ancient cash register. The hunk of metal jumped and popped open, sounding as if somebody had just slammed a meter maid between a pair of giant cymbals. He pulled a napkin from the drawer and slid it across the bar to Hobbs. Next to the phone number the name Junior was scrawled.

"You think I should hear him out?" asked Hobbs.

"I think you should fucking retire already, Hobbsy. But that's fuck all. The question is, what do you think?"

Hobbs slid the napkin back across the bar. "Tell him to meet me."

"Where?"

Hobbs told him. They talked about the details of the meet for a while, then Hobbs flipped a twenty out on the bar and left.

EIGHT

When Hobbs had asked how he'd recognize the kid, Cleary asked him, "Did ye ever find Waldo?"

Hobbs shook his head.

"Nothing? You've never read *Where's Waldo*?"

Hobbs had just looked at him.

"Ye've no children, or grandchildren or nieces or nephews?"

Hobbs hadn't changed his expression.

"Well it's a fine idea of livin' you've got for yourself if you don't mind me saying so."

"I don't like kids."

"How do you expect your memory will be preserved for posterity?"

"I don't. Now how will I know him?"

"Believe me, you'll know him, he's a regular fashion plate, this one. Besides, I'll tell him to find you. Just look for the dour old man who looks as out of place as a child molester."

"I don't like kids."

"Well, you've picked a hell of a place for it, then."

Hobbs had told Cleary he'd meet the kid on a bench in front of the entrance to the Wild One, the gigantic wooden roller coaster that cut right through the middle of Six Flags. Cleary had had a good laugh at that: "Amusement park. I said he was young, I didn't mean he was a *kid* kid."

So now Hobbs sat on a bench at Six Flags, surrounded by a never-ending stream of children. Their shrieks of delight and terror and their tantrums echoed from throughout the park. And he sat through all of it. In his gray work pants and white shirt, he was out of place, as if he had been left there from a time when the park ran in black and white. Every so often he mopped at the sweat on his neck and forehead.

He spotted the kid immediately. A punk, and a rich punk at that. Skinny jeans that looked like leggings, hat on sideways, a *knit* cap even though it was ninety goddamn degrees out here, and horizontally red-and-white-striped shirt. Freak show. Hobbs almost got up and walked away right then and there. But there was something about the way the kid walked. As if he was in on a secret that nobody else knew. Hobbs stayed put.

The kid sat next to him. He nodded hello, and then looked away as if he were waiting for someone else. Then he dug in his messenger bag and asked no one in particular, "Is your smart-phone encrypted?"

"I don't have a phone. Wrong end of the leash," said Hobbs.

Alan looked up sharply, losing his cool for a moment. Didn't have a phone! But he reeled it back in quickly.

"I go see people. I talk to them. They call people. Then I talk to them to see how the call went," said Hobbs.

"But for, like, friends, don't you ever call friends? Or Facebook, like Facebook friends?"

"A friend is somebody who comes by to visit every once in a while; everybody else is just an asshole who wastes your time," said Hobbs.

Alan let this sink in. "Well, good," he blustered, trying to get to his original point. "'Cause that tower over there"—he nodded his chin to the cell tower silhouetted against the sky behind the Wild One—"it's a fake. NSA or somebody dummied it up to practice cracking phones."

He held up his phone. On the screen it read, "Unencrypted connection. Caution: The mobile network's standard encryption has been turned off, possibly by a rogue base station ('unknown')." Alan continued smugly, "Anybody in this park, well, let's just say all their nudie pictures belong to somebody else now."

"Let's ride the ride," said Hobbs.

"You like roller coasters?" asked Alan with a snicker.

"No," said Hobbs.

As they shuffled through the endless line, Alan tried to start a serious conversation, about the job. About what he could do for Hobbs.

"Save it," was all Hobbs said.

By the luck of the draw, they were placed in the first car on the roller coaster. As the padded bar dropped over them, Hobbs said, "Let me see your phone." Alan handed it over, confident that no force on earth could defeat its encryption. Hobbs called out to the guy working the ride. "Hey!" As soon as the guy looked, Hobbs tossed him the phone. The attendant bobbled it twice, then got it under control. "Hang on to that," Hobbs said as the ride started.

"What the fuck? That's my phone."

"I don't like being recorded. And I don't like taking chances."

As the roller coaster picked up speed, Alan was forced to yell into the wind, "My phone is secure from all that shit."

"Yeah, but I don't trust *you*."

"Why should you?" asked Alan.

Hobbs smiled as the roller coaster chugged up the big hill at the start. As the first car went over the edge, and the coaster picked up speed, Hobbs said, "Give it to me."

Alan did, as quickly as possible, pausing only when the coaster swung them around one of the sharper curves. An armored car full of cash, benefit payments, still made in cash to poor folks along the Florida Panhandle. The rest, cash paid to contractors working in and around Eglin Air Force Base.

When they got off the ride, Hobbs asked, "You sellin' or you want in?"

"I want in."

Hobbs opened his mouth to say something and closed it again, afraid that what was going to come out wouldn't be words. Goddamned roller coasters.

"Are you OK?" asked Alan.

"No," said Hobbs.

"You look a little green."

He leaned heavily on Alan, putting an arm around his shoulders. Then he held Alan in place as he threw up on the kid's five-hundred-dollar sneakers. When he recovered himself he said, "I'm gonna look into it. If it checks out, I'll be in Saint Louis in a week. Chase Park Plaza Hotel. I'll be there as Ronald Caspar. Meet me."

"Don't you have a cell phone, or an e-mail address or something? I mean, what if it doesn't check out? What if you change your mind? I mean, what is in Saint Louis? I would have wasted a trip."

"Get a new pair of shoes," said Hobbs. Then he walked away, wiping his mouth with the back of his hand.

Neither of them stopped to look at the pictures of the last run of the roller coaster. A crowd gathered to laugh at the faces twisted in horror and delight as they flashed up on the screen. As the coaster had passed over the biggest drop on the run, the camera had captured Hobbs and Alan locked in conversation. While everyone else behind them was wide eyed and/or screaming, their eyes were locked on each other's. It looked as if they were preparing to fight to the death in the middle of a plane crash.

NINE

Stomach still shaky, Hobbs pulled out of Six Flags and drove south. Two days later he was in Tallahassee.

Hobbs checked into a hotel and made a call from the lobby phone. He confused the desk clerk when he asked for a phone book, but after he described the item and its function, the clerk was able to dig one up.

Hobbs looked up a number, called, left a message, and went to sleep. A few hours later, the phone started ringing. Hobbs sat up in the darkened room, coughed hard, and got it on the fifth ring. “Yeah.”

“Why, Hobbs, what a pleasant surprise it was to get your call and to hear your voice,” said Lester Broyles Jr. in an accent that sounded as Southern, dipped in shit, and confident as if this slippery fucker had won the Civil War single-handedly.

“I’ve got something for you,” said Hobbs.

“Your message said as much. And as little. Perhaps you could tell me even less,” Broyles said with a false chuckle.

“Yeah,” said Hobbs, not liking the way he was being toyed with, but what else was he gonna do? He didn’t know how to steal money, real money, without money. If ever he figured that one out, he’d really be free.

“Well, come by for dinner this evening, and you can tell me nothing about it. Besides, Darlene would love to see you.”

Broyles was a hustler from a long ways back, a criminal defense attorney in Louisiana who had been working angles for as long as Hobbs had known him. Hobbs had used him to finance three jobs. None of the jobs had come off without a hitch. The third had seemed good, but gone sour at the split. Broyles had insisted on being there, which meant it was his fault he'd gotten shot.

In the scramble after the two men who had taken the money, all turned against all. Somewhere in there, Hobbs stashed Broyles in a closet. When Hobbs was the last man standing, he went back for him. Surprised to find Broyles still alive, he took him to a veterinarian who did an off-the-books side business in gunshot wounds. Hobbs even left Broyles with his cut.

Hobbs didn't have any illusions about friendship or gratitude. He was pretty sure that Broyles wouldn't have bothered to drag him into a closet—or give him his share—but money men who kept their mouths shut weren't easy to find. Hobbs hadn't thought it wise to thin the herd.

After that he had heard that Broyles had moved to Miami and made a big score. The word was he had retired, but when Hobbs heard that Broyles had gotten elected to the Florida House of Representatives from some tiny, shit-poor district, Hobbs began to think that Broyles hadn't retired. He'd gone pro.

The guy's house in Tallahassee was a fucking mansion. A long, tree-lined drive with Spanish moss hanging from the branches and everything. While someone worked hard preparing dinner somewhere, Hobbs, Broyles, and his much younger wife, Darlene, sat on the porch and sipped bourbon. No mint for Hobbs. None of that julep nonsense.

"Hobbs," Broyles said after they had dispensed with all the bullshit and the pleasantries, "your problem isn't that you are a criminal, it's that you think too small. Politics, that's where the real money is. Why, they pay you just to vote. I swear, I should have done this years ago. It even would have been worth the effort. I am as happy as a protractor in a room full of angles. As happy as swarm of ticks on a moist dog's asshole."

"Honey!" said Darlene. "That's just foul." Hobbs hadn't smiled at Broyles's colorful analogies, but he did smile at Darlene. She had been a pretty girl who had grown into a beautiful woman. She had been a cheerleader at LSU, which, as Broyles was fond of reminding everyone, was home to the prettiest girls of any college in the United States. It would have been a mistake to think that she was a trophy wife. It was a professional relationship, and a good one. She rode Broyles the way a jockey rides a racehorse. If he faltered in his rise to wealth and power, she would find another horse. That simple.

Hobbs wondered how much of Broyles's success was due to this woman who sipped something that wore a frilly umbrella as a hat and asked, "So what excitement have you brought us this time, Mr. Hobbs? Has he told you, dear?"

"Why, no, honey, we were still exchanging the pleasantries."

"Pleasantries, are they? Mr. Hobbs, please don't let me deprive you of the pleasantries of a moist dog's asshole." She pronounced every word carefully and crisply, her eyes glittering brightly as she did. Hobbs raised his drink to her and sipped.

"We can skip the pleasantries," said Hobbs.

"You see, honey, that's what I like about this man," Broyles said, a little too loudly. "He's not from around here. Damn Yankee, get right to the point, and amen to that."

They all drank.

"It's an armored car," said Hobbs.

Broyles chuckled. Darlene just shook her head and smiled.

"You haven't heard it yet," said Hobbs.

"Why, Hobbs, I am surprised at you. Is this you pining for the old days? It's no good. You said it yourself not long ago, they're just like banks, they've gotten to where they ain't worth the effort."

"What I said was, the risk wasn't worth the payoff. This is a very big payoff."

"How much?"

Hobbs told him.

"Why, Mr. Hobbs," said Darlene, suddenly a little breathless, "you have seized my attention."

Hobbs held her gaze and said, "It's just Hobbs."

"First name or last?" Darlene asked, toying with him.

"Just Hobbs."

When she looked away, Broyles said, "Run it for me. What's the setup? Who's the finger? And spare no detail about the part where you will overcome the onboard telemetry, et cetera, et cetera."

Hobbs unfolded a Florida state map.

"You know, they have maps on computers now. And they make very impressive presentation and sales tools," said Broyles.

Hobbs traced a route out of Tallahassee south to the coast, through Carrabelle, Apalachicola and Panama City. Before he could say anything, Broyles burst into laughter.

"My God, how could I have missed it?"

Darlene asked, "Missed what?"

"I could have fingered this job. Isn't that funny? I have recently been appointed to the Appropriations Subcommittee on General Government. The great State of Florida is a wondrous and many-tentacled thing, so, among other things, the subcommittee includes payments and disbursements for those less fortunate. In my district a number of those people do not have bank accounts. In fact, throughout the Florida Panhandle, many people still get paid in cash. Fishermen, oystermen, maintenance workers. It is a very rural part of the country, after all. And with the Tyndall and Eglin Air Force Bases, well, you know how young men like to spend money on vices. Can't have a record of that, now can we?

"So, naturally, I was very curious about these funds." He changed his voice, to make it sound deeper and more statesman-like. "We have a fiduciary responsibility to the people of the great State of Florida to ensure that not one penny is wasted or lost due to the commission of a fraudulent act, or by omission of some act of faith and diligence it is within our power to perform."

Hobbs rolled his eyes.

"He's a natural at this," said Darlene.

"He's an orator, all right," Hobbs said. "They never get to the point."

"That's how I can tell you that last week there was twenty-three million dollars in there."

Hobbs froze. He held his glass of bourbon halfway from the table to his lips. Darlene's laugh rang out high and musical.

"My dear, now I think *you* have *his* attention."

Broyles finished his julep, sucking at his teeth. "If you can figure out how it can be done, I'll finance for a double share. Do you have a plan, or are you just here on what we in government call a fact-finding mission?"

"The only person's time and money I'm spending right now is my own. I've got ideas how we might take it. Lemme finish the details."

Hobbs realized that Darlene was staring at him in a predatory way. She was younger than Broyles by at least ten years. She dressed classy, but Hobbs could see there was spice in her. Ringlets of thick black hair framed her face, offset by brilliant red lipstick. That was about all the makeup she wore. Beneath her raised eyebrows her brown, hazel-flecked eyes glittered like stolen diamonds.

Hobbs asked her stare, "What?"

"So you can do it?" Just a flicker of tongue between the gap in her front teeth.

"I want to," said Hobbs, with a shrug. "But it's not up to me right now. Have to see how it comes together."

"Don't let him fool you, darlin'. Mr. Hobbs's specialty is armored transport. There are countermeasures developed specifically to thwart techniques that this man invented. His innovation and audacity support a large part of the security industry. And since he declared that the game was over, ten years ago, there has not been a successful armored car robbery in the continental United States. Some may get away with the money, but they never quite get away with the crime. So if he is interested—if he says maybe—that's as good as a yes to me."

"You talk a lot," said Hobbs.

"And the richer and more powerful I become, the more people are forced to listen," said Broyles, handing his empty glass to Darlene.

TEN

Hobbs drove the route twice. Once following the truck, the next scouting all the likely places for a grab. He used an old Polaroid to take pictures of anything he thought might be useful. Any angle that might play. The film was expensive, and harder and harder to get—but the one thing you knew with a Polaroid was that the picture you held in your hand was the only one. When you burned it, it was gone forever.

He was going to take another pass at the route, mostly just to think while driving, but that night, exhaustion got to him. When he was younger, he could go a long time without sleep while working and still stay sharp. He had spent most of his off time lazing around in the sun, like some kind of predator. But when the hunt was on, he had been tireless. Those days were long gone. In the time between those days and now, Miami had gone from a paradise to a slum, then back again. In the old days he had stayed in the finest hotels and on the finest women.

Hobbs stopped at a supermarket in Carrabelle, then pulled into the old motor court next door. The lady behind the counter was weathered and had a face like an oyster shell. She showed him to a room in the back.

The window unit whined and struggled against the heat of a Florida night that was never going to cool off. Hobbs pored over the map and made notes on a yellow pad. Then he went to the half fridge and got a can of beer. He held it to his head for a moment. Then he opened it, drank deeply, and sat down again.

It was a nightmare. Hobbs remembered when armored cars had become more trouble than they were worth. A crew he knew of got sent up because of a hidden GPS tracker in the early nineties. Before that, GPS had been fifty-pound military monstrosities that couldn't be hidden. And there had been no way to get information out of them easily. But a GPS hooked to a cell phone? The company called it and it very kindly told the company where its truck was. Poor bastards got busted at the split.

Hobbs had gone to visit one of them in prison to get the whole story. But never mind the particulars, this business of taking things from their rightful owners had been getting harder and harder. Or maybe Hobbs was just too damn old for it anymore. Still, $23 million was a pile of cash. Used to be you could knock off an armored car with three guys. Three guys plus two shares for Broyles…4.6 million apiece. Launder it, at worst fifty cents on the dollar, 2.3 million.

Hobbs took off his glasses. He rubbed his eyes and thought, *That's a good number to go out on. I could put up a number like that and be done, couldn't I?*

But how to do it? These armadillos had gone high tech. Sure, it was driving through the middle of goddamned lonely nowhere, but now it would have better telemetry on it than *Apollo 13*. The minute something went wrong, the central office would know about it. To say nothing of the onboard cameras. Even if you took the truck, the company would be on it before you could unload the money.

Supposedly it even had a helicopter on standby anytime the truck got too far out of civilization. That was from a Moonis-Brainerd brochure, so it was probably bullshit. Hobbs might be a thief, but thank God he wasn't in marketing. Those were some lying bastards.

There hadn't been any of the gadgets and radios and devices and gizmos before. Before, phones had cords and men had courage. A strong, smart guy who was good under pressure could make a dishonest living. Or an honest one. If you knew a trade, you'd have work. Now everybody grew up dreaming of middle management.

Hobbs saw himself as a tradesman. He'd first broken bad as a supply sergeant. Southeast Asia was a bumpy place. Lots of things fell off trucks. And the way Hobbs looked at it, the start of those police actions had been the start of the corporate wars. All the bullshit. Now you couldn't call anything what it was. *Police action, preemptive strike*—hell, they even changed the name of the War Department to the Department of Defense. Bullshit all around. That's when the news became obsessed with casualty stats. That's when the bean counters took over.

In the end Hobbs saw that everybody was in it to grab what they could for themselves. The way he saw it, that left him two choices. Go crazy, or start grabbing. He chose to make a buck.

But he hadn't paid off the right people. So when he stepped on the big kids' toes by sending a shipment of heroin back from Cambodia to the Bronx, it all came crashing down on him. Bad conduct discharge, back to the States. Luckily he was in it deep enough that they couldn't really charge him without bringing down their own con, so he was left more or less to his own devices.

Hobbs had taken half his stash, bought three new identities from a round guy in Seattle, and gone to work in earnest. His real name had been lost in the mists of history. He had left his original identity behind so long ago, he wasn't entirely sure that his memories were real anymore. He didn't have any friends from back then. He didn't like to think about his family. No photographs, no mementos. For Hobbs, his work was everything. He was a craftsman in a rough trade, but a perfectible one.

As he sat with the map and the pad, it felt as if he had come to the end of it. He couldn't see a way to make this one work. Maybe the days of the heavy heist were gone for good.

At times he would get glimpses of things that might have been his past, but he never trusted them. Not memories, exactly. More like images, sounds, smells. He really trusted only the smells.

Once, while driving through the night, racing away from a job that had gone wrong, he had scented a copse of pine trees after a spring rain. That smell called forth an image of his grandfather shaving. A towel wrapped around the bottom of his thin and withered body. His jackal's smile through the brush-lathered foam. "Aye, c'mere and see how it's done. Make a man of ye, razor cuts and all." The accent was improbably Irish. But that was the sound part. He didn't trust it. For all Hobbs knew, that line was just a memory implanted from a late-night movie he had fallen asleep to. But with it was the smell of a cigarette burning on the edge of the sink. Even now he could see the old man close his lips around the filter, suck, and pull it away, leaving lather on the brown paper.

He shook off the smoke of memory and got up out of the chair. Halfway to the fridge, he looked back at the pad as if it were a man who had just spit an insult at him and needed to be knocked down. There was always another problem, a knot to be unwound or cut clean through, before a job could be completed. He just couldn't see this one, not yet. But he had to find a way. If he didn't, then what was he?

He opened another beer and drank from it, not taking his eyes from the papers on the table. He'd be goddamned if it didn't feel like the end of something. Of it. Of all of it. Was he obsolete?

Another memory. A girl he had shacked up with in the seventies. They sat naked under a blanket on the porch of a ramshackle house overlooking the port of Oakland. Klieg lights casting an unholy light across the run-down end of the city at three o'clock in the morning. Down there, in the footlights of the apocalypse, a crew labored to get a ship ready for sea. Hobbs was fresh off a job in Seattle, trying to rob that port of bullion. He had lost the bullion, but had gotten away with his life and enough to buy a train ticket south. It hadn't taken him long to shack up with a stripper working in San Francisco but living cheap in Oakland.

When she first asked him what he did, he said import-export. But later, in the wee small hours, sitting on the porch, he told her. She fired up a joint and said, "No shit," in a way that meant *I think you're full of shit.*

She offered him the joint. He didn't take it. He looked at her through the thin trail of funny-smelling smoke being carried out to sea by the land breeze.

She said, "'Good shutting makes no use of bolt or bar, yet no one can undo it.'" Then she asked him if he knew what that was. "It's the Tao," she said, before she took another hit. Her voice squeaked as she said, "Eastern wisdom, real heavy."

That was the exact moment Hobbs had decided to leave the West Coast for good. Between the busted job in Seattle and this ex-hippie stripper, he had had enough. Until right now, he had never thought of that girl again. How strange that he couldn't remember her name and yet that crazy quote was still there.

He flipped to a fresh page on the pad and wrote the words down very carefully in the middle. "Good shutting makes no use of bolt or bar..." Like a fucking riddle. What about the opposite? What was good opening? Good opening made no use of...He felt the urge to research the truck, or the company that made the telemetry system. He recognized it as the impulse of fear that it was. There'd be time enough for that later. Right now it would just be a distraction.

The problem was clear enough. An armored truck on a lonely road along the "Forgotten Coast." A ping—like a heartbeat letting the lords and masters know that the cash was still theirs and on course. Two to three men on board at the start of a long day scattering cash throughout the panhandle.

Scenario after scenario ran through his mind. Even if they cracked the armadillo and got away from the site, there were too few people and too few ways out of those empty spaces on the map. The whole area was just too thin. They'd be too easily spotted. Especially if the armored car company had the helicopter support it boasted of in its glossy brochure.

He stared at the pad, feeling blurry and weak. It sure felt like the end of it. Of *him*. He wanted a cigarette. He wanted to shave. He wanted to have been an electrician like his grandfather. (Had that even been true? Did it matter?)

He inserted himself between the scratchy sheets and turned out the light. He tried to sleep. But those crazy words wouldn't let go of him.

Shutting. Bolt. Bar.

Everything moved so fast now. Everything was always on, always available. Hobbs was a guy who didn't even have a cell phone. He didn't like carrying around a tracking device. But who needed the damn things anyway? He didn't know how to be faster than the spin of the modern world. *You can't be faster,* he told himself, *you're too old and raggedy.* All he had was slow.

Opening. Key.

Good stealing makes no use of...yet no one can stop it.

And then he had the answer.

The next day he went to see Broyles and told him how much he'd need to put the job together. It was a hefty sum, but Broyles didn't bat an eye. He went in the back. Darlene flirted with Hobbs for a while. And when Broyles came back, he handed Hobbs a suitcase filled with cash. That's what trust got you in this business. But then, trust also got you killed.

Broyles said, "I'd like that briefcase back, if you don't mind." Hobbs saw he was serious. Strange bird.

ELEVEN

From Tallahassee he drove north into Georgia. If he was going to pull this off he was going to need help, and equipment. Even if he took that kid from the roller coaster as ballast—and that was a big if—he'd still need somebody he could depend on. A pro. The job would also need some iron. Not much, but still. And he knew where he could find both.

He drove through the center of Georgia, past mile after mile of pecan trees that were already withering in the early heat of spring. Hobbs wondered why anybody would feel the need to fight a war over this land. Hot, ugly, and empty. But you could say similar things about Korea, or Afghanistan.

He paralleled the Chattahoochee River and the Georgia-Alabama border. Ahead of him, like a colossus, lay the sprawling expanse of Fort Benning, and beyond it Columbus, Georgia. Two miles short of Columbus was a town called Lumpkin. It was a small town built around a courthouse. A county seat like a thousand other dying little towns in the South. Only this one had thrived by grabbing on to the past with both hands and holding tight.

Signs pointed toward Westville. Like Gettysburg, this was a reconstruction of a historical town. Hobbs went the opposite way on Main Street. He wasn't interested in the past.

On the far end of Main Street was a joint that was open only for breakfast and lunch. The ancient Pepsi sign read "Jimmy's

Bar-B-Que," but everybody called it by the current owner's name: Hurlocker's.

Hobbs pushed through the door and back about twenty years. The place had a shotgun layout, one side filled with a counter and a short-order kitchen. On the other side, tucked underneath the stairs that went from the street to the top level, were booths of dark wood. The floor was faded red tile, set in a diamond pattern around smaller black tiles, all pleasantly slick with grease. Behind the counter one of four deep-fat fryers roared, hot oil and bubbles working their magic on some unknown piece of food. Did it matter? Even if you deep-fried shipping peanuts, they'd be delicious.

A yell came from behind the silver swinging door with the porthole window that led to the back: "We're closed!" Hobbs ignored it and sat at the counter. The chipped Formica top was so old it could probably remember a time when only white people were allowed to sit at it. "I ain't heard nobody leave yet!" the voice from the back came again.

Hobbs waited.

The silver doors banged into the wall as a huge man wearing an apron limped into the room. Hurlocker looked like a hairy vulture. Long neck, wide arms, shoulders so broad it looked as if he had to stoop to get through a door. He never gave the appearance of being in a hurry, but Hobbs had seen him move fast enough when required. Hurlocker unfurled his long arms and put his palms on the counter. "Hobbs," he said, naming him without any warmth.

Without taking his eyes off Hobbs, Hurlocker reached under the counter and produced a coffee cup and pot of coffee. He filled the cup and set it in front of Hobbs.

"Business, pleasure, or both?" asked Hurlocker.

Hobbs asked, "Both? What's both?"

Hurlocker laid a finger against his beak of a nose. "Re-venge, Hobbs, re-venge."

Hobbs sipped the coffee and made a face. It was as bitter as regret. "Business," he said.

"Always business with you, eh? Leroy! Quit pullin' your pork and git out here."

A wiry black man shuffled in from the back wearing an apron and holding a scrub brush.

"You remember Leroy, don't you, Hobbs?"

Leroy. Full name Elroy Church. A black man with one eye on the stars and one eye off to the left. He didn't walk right, and was plagued by tremors. To look at him, you'd think he was simple. You'd be wrong.

Twenty years back, Hobbs and Hurlocker had worked a job in upstate New York. Hurlocker had driven past the entrance to a VA hospital and whom had he seen sitting out front, shivering his black ass off in rags in the middle of a goddamned snowdrift, but Sergeant Elroy Church, forcibly retired? Hurlocker hadn't said a word. Just doubled back, driven the car right up to the drift, and put him in the back.

His only explanation was, "Not leavin' a man behind." Hobbs thought Hurlocker had gone off his goddamned rocker. But when the story came out, he understood, a little bit at least.

The story went that Leroy had saved Hurlocker's life twice in 'Nam. Both times on patrol. But it was in the city that Leroy caught his. A bomb went off in the whorehouse he was in, in Saigon. Didn't give him so much as a scratch, but the overpressure scrambled his brains. It was his ticket out. His unit thought he was gonna be fine, he had the VA and his people to take care of him. It wasn't until New York, years later, that Hurlocker knew any different.

On this New York job, the third man, an explosives guy named Hargett, had tried to cross them. He had nearly pulled it off. But he hadn't paid attention to the simple cripple they had brought along as a mascot. Steady as a rock, Leroy had picked up a pistol and shot Hargett in the eye from across the room. "Boy," he'd said to Hurlocker, "I ain't saving you no fourth time." When Leroy had made sure that Hargett was dead, his tremors had started again.

The shake and the limp and one of the eyes were no act. Those parts of his brain had been rearranged, but the rest was just fine. Leroy liked playing dumb, and getting all the advantages he could from his misfortune. In fact, he had been setting up on the VA hospital when they picked him up. His plan had been to rob it of all the opiates he could get his hands on. Had the whole deal wired, fence and all. So after Hargett was dead, they went on and looted the VA pharmacy as a victory lap.

Hurlocker had been looking after Leroy ever since. Or maybe it was the other way around. When Hobbs asked him about it, Hurlocker had made light of it, saying, "The minute he starts shittin' himself, I'm gonna take him out back and shoot him. I ain't changin' no goddamned diapers."

They all settled into a booth and Hobbs laid the whole thing out for them. Asked if they wanted in.

"Tha's r-r-r-real nice, Hobbs. I didn't think you was h-h-h-half that clever," said Leroy.

Hobbs smiled. "I just thought to myself, Leroy's sneaky. What would he do?"

"Don't f-f-f-flatter me none," said Leroy. "I'm too old to go runnin' off on any job. 'Sides, I got myself a lady."

"She ain't no lady," said Hurlocker.

"He jes-jes' jealous. He ain't been g-g-g-g-gettin' any for a while."

"How would you know?"

"I s-s-s-see you lookin' at me when I bend over to pull that pig. You got that g-g-g-gleam in your eye."

"I got some on the side you don't know about," protested Hurlocker. They went on like an old married couple for a while.

Hobbs let them run and then asked, "You in?"

"I'm too old for all that nonsense," said Leroy.

Hurlocker looked over at him and said, "See, now he's talkin' sense for once. You'd do well to take it easy, Hobbs. Enjoy your golden years."

"I enjoy gold," said Hobbs. "You did too, once upon a time."

"Naw, naw," Hurlocker said, "I'm all gone to seed." He slapped his belly. "Too much beer has eaten all the profits. 'Sides, I can't leave him to run the store."

Leroy tremored a little harder as he twisted in the booth and hit Hurlocker in the shoulder. "You think I cain't handle it? That maybe I'd steal from you?"

"Why, no. If this place made more money while I was gone, you'd never let me hear the end of it! Not in a million years would you let that shit go."

Leroy smiled and twitched, blurring a little with happiness.

"All right, then," said Hurlocker, thinking he was changing the subject, "where's my manners? You need something to eat. You look like you been drivin' about a week.

"You haven't said whether you're in or not," said Hobbs.

"No," said Hurlocker with a smile, "I haven't. But you ain't said if you want something to eat."

Hobbs said, "Sure, I'll take some barbecue. But I also need some of the other."

Hurlocker smiled. "Well then, let's go have a peek in the ol' Hurt Locker."

The place was a real restaurant. Hurlocker handled the short-order cooking and public relations while Leroy tended the smokers out back, turning out barbecue that was so well-loved they hardly ever had leftovers. In and of itself, it was a profitable little operation. Hobbs couldn't have done it. He didn't like people. And he hated cooking.

Hurlocker led Hobbs into the back. On the right, stairs descended into the basement. It was filled with a musty, clammy smell. The thick Georgia clay locked in the moisture. There were wire shelves with supplies for the restaurant, and a large walk-in freezer in the far corner.

Hurlocker picked up an ancient eight-pound ball-peen hammer off one of the shelves. "Been a while since I had any customers in the showroom," he explained as he opened the freezer.

Inside, a side of beef lay on the floor. It was frozen into two inches of ice and surrounded by thick frost stalagmites. Hurlocker grabbed it and pulled. When it didn't budge, he hooked a hand under it and pounded away. Chips of ice exploded into the air, and soon his hammer rang on steel decking. Within a few minutes he had broken the beef free and slid it to the center of the room.

Where the beef had been was a trap door. As Hurlocker battered the edge of the door and the hinges he said, "Been meaning to get a blowtorch for this..." He pulled the door back and descended a metal ladder.

Beneath the freezer was a cement-walled room stretching the width of the freezer and the length of the building. The walls were lined with pegboard, and on the pegboard was a treasure trove of untraceable weapons. Below the pegboard, rifle cases were stacked up around the perimeter, five and six high.

"Shop is open," said Hurlocker. "What you need?"

"Who the fuck buys that?" Hobbs asked, pointing to a surface-to-air missile on the far wall.

"Lots of folk. Them that's nervous about the second War of Northern Aggression. People with an overdeveloped sense of privacy. Some as just wants to make an impression at the Fourth of July. So, AKs?" he asked, pointing to a wall of Kalashnikovs in many configurations. "I got stamped receiver and, for a little extra, milled. Totally untraceable."

Hobbs said, "I like your enthusiasm, but we're not going to invade a country. Things go right, who's gonna need to fire a shot?"

"Better to have and not need, than need and not have."

Hobbs rubbed his eyes. After years of this kind of thing, it was getting old. At least he wasn't dealing with an asshole. Hurlocker would charge him the arm, but not the leg, and he wouldn't fuck around as he did it.

Hobbs picked six revolvers, in .38 and .40 calibers. Hurlocker made a joke about size and limited firepower. Hobbs said, "You're welcome to bring whatever you want on this job, just so long as it isn't that missile."

Hurlocker smiled that versatile smile of his and said, "Didn't you hear Leroy? He was talkin' sense."

"Was he talkin' your kind of sense?"

Hurlocker looked around the room a good long time. "This thing ain't even proper fingered yet. You gonna take a chance on this kid?"

"No," said Hobbs. "I don't think he has any sand anyway. We'll see in Saint Louis."

"Saint Louis," said Hurlocker, drawing *Louis* out to about three syllables in his south Georgia accent. "That's one shitty town."

Hobbs said nothing.

"Well, I just wouldn't feel right about letting a little fella like you head up there all alone."

"OK," said Hobbs, putting an end to it.

"No, I'm serious, if I let you go up there and something were to happen to you—well, Leroy, I mean, there'd be no living with him."

They wrapped the guns in plastic bags and put them into Styrofoam to-go containers. In the kitchen Leroy ladled a little barbecue into each, saying, "For the smell. Shame to waste it, though."

When Hurlocker went up front to grab some cash from the register, Leroy grabbed Hobbs's shoulder with surprising strength. "You sure you know your business? You sure you need this business? You're too old for this." His one good eye was wide and accusing.

Hobbs said, "I'm too old for anything else."

"I'm serious, now. If it don't look right, don't force it."

From the doorway Hurlocker said, "Christ on a crutch, Leroy, just 'cause that one wonky eye looks like it can see into the future don't mean you should act like it does."

Leroy didn't look at Hurlocker. He said, "That one ain't got no sense. You got sense. You don't let it go sideways."

"I'll do what I can," said Hobbs, annoyed that Leroy had gone so soft that he'd even think to say such a thing.

TWELVE

There were twenty-three companies licensed to build and upgrade armored cars in the United States. Most of them were newcomers, specializing in discreetly armored vehicles for executives and government officials and members of regimes, cartels, and organizations so crooked that they had people fighting to be first in line for a chance to kill them. Business for these companies was booming, and not all their production was shipped out of the country.

Regent Armored in Saint Louis, Missouri, was not one of this kind of company. A family-owned business, it had been one of the primary suppliers to couriers like Securitas, Brink's and Moonis-Brainerd. But this is not to suggest that business was bad. On the contrary, business was stable and profitable. Making new armored cars is, by nature, a pretty limited business. Armored cars are designed to be impervious. Because of their requirements, they don't conform well to schemes of planned obsolescence. And they can't be made more attractive through cost-cutting measures. Cold rolled steel costs what it costs, and that is that.

Daniel McCaffery, the patriarch in charge of Regent, knew this. That's why he had focused on transferring existing armor to new chassis. All the weight quickly wore out engines, drivetrains, and suspensions. McCaffery had figured out how to make this refurb business so profitable that he sold new armored cars for less than it cost to make them, with the provision that he was contracted to get the refurb when it came due.

The majority of the Brink's truck–style armored carriers in the United States made the pilgrimage to Saint Louis to be refurbished. It was nothing less than the Fountain of Youth for armored cars.

From the roof of the abandoned factory across the street, three men watched a semi pull three armored cars into Regent Armored's facility. The facility was an up-fitted Art Deco brick building that looked antique on the outside, but through the gigantic sliding door they could see that it was pristine, well-lit, and state of the art on the inside.

"Glad I don't work there," said Alan. Hurlocker passed the binoculars to Hobbs. Neither of them acknowledged the whiny kid when he added, "Glad I don't work," with a nasty little giggle. The kid opened his laptop, a powerful, custom-built gaming PC that he had once devoted to the Universe of Strife. It was a few years out of date as far as gaming went, but its powerful processor, twin onboard graphics cards, and high-resolution screen made it plenty fast enough for the hackery he needed on this job. His fingers flew across the keyboard, and a detailed blueprint of the building appeared on the screen.

"You guys want a closer look? Here are the plans," he said triumphantly.

Hobbs looked over his shoulder to where Alan hunched in the pea gravel with his shiny laptop. "It's not the parts that don't move that we need to worry about. It's the people that are going to be your problem."

"What do mean? You mean I'm going to steal the truck? I'm in this thing as the tech guy. I'm not, not a…you know, a…"

"You're not in this thing at all," said Hobbs. "You want in? This is an *audition*. You're a guy I don't know and nobody I know knows you. So I gotta find some way to know."

"But this isn't the job. These trucks don't have any money in them!" said Alan.

"This is the job so we can do the job. He doesn't get it," Hobbs said to Hurlocker. "Maybe you can explain it to him."

"It ain't exactly clear that we speak the same language," said Hurlocker, not looking at Alan.

"Hey, that's not friendly," said Alan. Hobbs and Hurlocker looked at Alan as if he were crazy. Then Hurlocker turned back to the binos.

Hurlocker said, "I make twelve guys total. Don't know if they run a third shift, but we can call this second shift."

"What are we stealing?" asked Alan, peering up over the wall to take a look at the problem in the real world for the first time.

"Not us," said Hobbs, "you."

"But I'm not a..."

"What? What aren't you? What are you? That's what we are here to figure out. You don't want to do it. That's fine. You go back to Philadelphia. We'll give you a share if the job comes off. You want to be a thief, you're gonna steal one of those armored cars for us."

"Can I see the binoculars?"

Hurlocker passed them. Alan scanned the whole building. He looked a long, long time. Then he said, "So, just boost one of those big trucks. Like boosting any other car."

"Just steal the truck," said Hobbs.

"But not like any other car," said Hurlocker. "With another vehicle you'd be able to run for it like a spooked moonshiner. But with one of these big sombitches, you gotta get away clean, or they'll chase you. And if they chase you, they'll catch you. So no hurting people, no triggering alarms, nothing. All very professional and untraceable. Like a movie—if it's the most boring movie you've ever seen."

"What are they doing in there? All those sparks?" Alan asked, still looking through the binos.

Hobbs said, "They're putting old truck bodies on new chassis. New engines, new springs, new everything."

"OK, which one you want?" asked Alan.

"Doesn't matter, just make sure you steal one that runs."

Alan handed the binoculars back to Hobbs. "OK, let's do it."

Hurlocker smiled a pained smile and looked away.

"Kid," said Hobbs.

"Seriously, why fuck around? I'm gonna go steal a truck. Right now."

Hurlocker said, "Got to love a game rooster," in a way that suggested he really didn't love this one.

"Well then, fuck you. You steal it."

"Easy. *Easy!*" said Hobbs. "Look, there's a right way and a wrong way. A lotta wrong ways. There are steps to this dance, and we're gonna show you."

"So what's the next step?"

"We wait. We watch. We take notes. We—"

"That doesn't sound like the next-level, badass shit I signed up for."

Hobbs rubbed his eyes. "You didn't sign up. You applied. And you haven't been accepted yet." He threw down a composition book and a pen. "Take notes, you've got the first watch."

Alan looked at the pen and paper as if they were something from the Jurassic period. "You want me to sit here and just watch."

"Eight-hour shifts, you've got the first one."

"In the middle of the night? But I won't get any sleep."

Hurlocker chuckled a low, wry chuckle. As he walked to the stairwell, he muttered, "I hate this town."

THIRTEEN

The next morning Hobbs and Hurlocker ate breakfast and went to the stakeout. When they got there, Alan wasn't on the roof. The notebook was there, but nothing was written in it.

"Well," said Hurlocker, "now we know."

Hobbs grunted and looked around.

Hurlocker said, "I wanted to catch him sleeping."

Hobbs said, "What difference would it have made?"

"Kicking the shit out of him would have served as my daily constitutional. Besides, you get to be my age," said Hurlocker with a grin, "you'll jump at any excuse to feel young again."

Hurlocker turned and walked to the stairs. Hobbs stayed a minute, looking out over Regent Armored. Five stories below him and across the vacant lot, ordinary men were filing in for their ordinary day of work. For a moment Hobbs envied them. Men who had a respectable trade, never worried about the law or the double cross. Then he rubbed his eyes and saw them for the tame creatures they were. He'd be bored out of his mind in a job like that. What was he going to do when it finally did come time to retire? Would such a thing even be possible? He shook it off. He wasn't retiring today. Today was all that mattered.

He caught up with Hurlocker in the stairwell. The rangy man was standing motionless, halfway down the flight of stairs, as if some movers had abandoned a wooden Indian. Then he turned and beckoned to Hobbs with one finger while he held the other to his lips. Hobbs closed the rooftop door gently and tiptoed down the stairs.

Hurlocker whispered, "You don't hear it?"

Hobbs shook his head.

Hurlocker whispered, "Hearing's the first thing to go."

Hobbs descended.

By the time they got to the fourth floor, Hobbs could hear it, a little at least. Music, high and tinny, no bass. And shitty music at that. Rap, hip-hop, some shit. He looked down and saw that Hurlocker had a pistol in his hand. He held it naturally, conversationally, as if it weren't a weapon, but maybe a flashlight that he would use to point out structural repairs in the crumbling building.

Hurlocker always did like guns too much, but he'd never been the trigger-happy sort. Hobbs had left his pistols where they belonged, in the trunk of the car. All the same, he eased out onto the floor quietly.

This floor had been a workshop of some kind. High ceilings, exposed timbers. In the corner was an office constructed of lath and plaster. At one time a foreman would have worked there, or maybe the plant manager. The door was closed, but the sound was definitely coming from in there. They picked their way through empty beer cans and spray paint, through trash, and over the grease marks and bolt holes where large machines had once been mounted to the floor.

They set up on either side of the door. Hurlocker held up three fingers and raised his eyebrows. Hobbs shook his head no. He tried the knob and the door swung easily. Hurlocker leaned around the jamb, fanned the room with the pistol, and leaned back. Relief flashed across his face, quickly replaced by disgust.

Hobbs looked for himself. Alan was asleep underneath a table. On top of the table were his laptop and some scattered gear.

Hobbs walked through the door and yelled, "Rise and shine!" Instead of jerking up and hitting his head as Hobbs had hoped,

Alan rolled over and said, "Oh, hey." Hurlocker stayed on the other side of the door.

"Well, you're fired."

"What are you talking about?"

"Sleeping on the job. Leaving your post. Fuck did you think was gonna happen?"

"I got it all," said Alan, rubbing his eyes, still not quite awake.

"You got it all my ass. You got nothing. The notebook is blank. You fail, kid."

"Notes? By hand? Are you shitting me? I took pictures."

"Pictures?" Hobbs said, turning around. "Best of luck, kid. Maybe you can get a job doing data entry on punch cards or something."

"*Hey!*" Alan yelled. He scampered up from the floor and blocked Hobbs's path, putting a pale, weak finger on Hobbs's chest. Behind him Hurlocker lifted his pistol and mimed bringing it down on the back of the kid's head. Hobbs shook his head no. He didn't mind the kid showing some grit. Even if this one was an idiot, it left some hope for future generations.

Alan said, "You're the asshole that wanted an audition, right? So let me show you what I can do."

"You showed me. You were asleep. I need guys I can count on."

"Job's done, jackass. Job's *been* done. And this? This is bullshit. This is a shitload of busywork just to show you what I'm capable of. But you're the jackass that wanted an audition. So let me audition."

Hobbs stared him down. Shitty music crackling away in the background, some kid yelling about bitches over a beat. It was a sound that should have been riding on twenty-two-inch rims rattling a trunk lid somewhere, rather than coming out of laptop speakers. Hobbs said, "Turn off that shitty music and show me what you've got."

Alan turned around and went right to the laptop. Next to the binoculars was a fancy digital camera with a long lens on it. Alan tapped some keys and a screenful of photos came up. They were a little grainy, but they didn't look as if they had been taken at night. They looked as if they could have been taken on a cloudy afternoon.

"I didn't take notes, you're right. I took pictures."

"Yeah, but what time did all that happen?" Hobbs asked as he watched the entire night play out in photos. Second shift going home. Third shift coming on. The doors opening to let the fresh summer night air in. A truck being finished and moved to the side lot.

"I've got time stamps on all of them." He fiddled with the computer and all the photos were displayed in a timeline. When he rolled over them, they zoomed to fill the top third of the screen.

Hurlocker was impressed in spite of himself. "That's one fancy notebook."

Alan held up a finger. "Just wait, my grim friend."

"I ain't your friend," said Hurlocker.

"Do you even have friends? Or is it just farm animals that can't outrun you anymore?"

Hobbs snickered and wished he hadn't.

"Boy, I got a gun."

"And a love for old, slow-moving sheep. Now watch this. See this guy right here?" He zoomed in on one picture of a man standing in the doorway, taking a break at about two forty-five. "This is Timothy Grahl, ASE-certified master mechanic. I picked him out using facial recognition technology and cross-referencing it with Facebook." He clicked and another window popped up, displaying a map. "This is where he lives."

"Wait, you're telling me this ol' boy has a Facebook page?" said Hurlocker.

"No, but his daughter does. Anyway, this is the complete list of everybody who was on shift last night," he said, clicking with a flourish. "Here's the complete employment records from the Missouri Department of Labor, Unemployment Security Division—I had to pay a guy to get these, so you're going to have to reimburse me."

"How much?" asked Hobbs.

"One bitcoin."

"What's a bitcoin?"

"Right now about two hundred and sixty-two US dollars, but that's not important. 'Cause after that, I really got to work. I couldn't hack into their security cameras for a real-time feed—that shit is for the movies—but I did get in through their router, and their cameras all transmit images via Wi-Fi. So I grabbed some from each camera…"

Views of the shop floor scrolled across the screen. "And I noticed something interesting."

He stopped on one image of a workbench and a wall. There was a time clock, and some fat guy was holding a strut and gas shock in the air, looking at the joint.

"What?" asked Hobbs.

"You don't see it? How about you, animal lover?" he asked with a smile, looking to Hurlocker. He shook his head no. "Ah come on, it's right there! I mean for a couple of hardened criminals like yourselves."

"Get on with it," said Hurlocker.

"You're no fun at all." Alan zoomed in. Next to the time clock was a lockbox with a keypad on it. "Bingo, key to every vehicle in the place, including the boss's new Benz. Not really my style, but the nicest car I've seen since I hit this shithole town."

"So?" asked Hurlocker.

"So then I wrote a little script to run a track on it. Pull a capture every half second. The combination is 75309." He looked over his shoulder at both of them. "So after that, I was tired. So I went to sleep. Oh wait, wait." He hit another key. "This is their project accounting software. It also handles shipping and receiving. So we don't even need to steal an armored car. You just tell me where you want it delivered and I'll have a bonded, third-party transport company drop it off. I just mark it as paid in their system and the fuck does the guy on the floor care?"

"Huh," said Hobbs. "Good job."

"Sure, you're tough in the real world, but I kick ass on the data layer, bitches," said Alan.

"Bitches?" Hobbs asked Hurlocker. Hurlocker's expression didn't change.

Alan said, "Now if you two Luddites will excuse me, I'm gonna go back to the hotel, shower the smell of this place off me, and get some sleep."

As Alan packed up his gear, Hobbs said to Hurlocker, "I hate to say it, but it's a good job."

Hurlocker nodded. "I still don't like him."

Hobbs said, "You're not the trusting kind."

Hurlocker shrugged. It could have meant *Sue me.* It could have meant *I don't give a fuck.* It could have meant anything.

Alan turned at the door. "Listen, if you guys just like hanging out in old buildings like a couple of crackhead hobos, that's fine with me. But when you're done, you just tell me where you want the truck delivered."

"It's not that easy, you still gotta steal it," said Hobbs.

"What are you talkin' about? I don't…I just told you! We can have it delivered like a fucking pizza. There's no need."

"We need the truck," said Hurlocker. "But we need to know you can handle yourself more."

"Oh, fuck you guys! Why you always gotta do things the hard way?"

"Not us," said Hurlocker, finally smiling. "You."

FOURTEEN

Hobbs drank coffee and watched Alan tear into a muffin like an animal. He was short on table manners, but Hobbs had stopped thinking he should have pushed him off that roller coaster. He wasn't a bad kid, just young and green and looking to prove something, most of all to himself. Those days were so far gone for Hobbs he could barely remember them.

The kid tried to make some small talk, but Hobbs touched a finger to his lips. "This isn't the part where you talk. This is the part where we be quiet." Alan shrugged and said, "OK, this is the part where I go sleep," and left. Hobbs watched him go. He wondered what it would have been like to have a kid of his own, a son. He tried to shake it off, but it wouldn't go.

It was Grace. She was the reason for every thought that tied him down. She held his life together in ways that he hadn't even known were possible. He had been some wild thing before he met her. He had been married, but that broad hadn't been any damn good. She'd had a bad loyalty gland and had killed herself from the guilt of betraying him. He had never figured out how a person could lack loyalty, but still feel guilt about it.

Hobbs was loyal to work. To the job. He was honest on the job, because that was the best way to get the job done.

After his wife was out of the picture, he had chopped his way through twenty jobs and twice as many women. He had been a shark. Swim, eat. Swim, fuck. Swim, eat. Swim, fuck. But always swimming. Always moving on.

Then came Grace. She had been on the arm of an idiot who had fingered a precious metals robbery. It had gone wrong, but when the dust had settled, she'd still been there. That first time, they'd coupled brutishly, with the reckless abandon of people freshly paroled by death. But for some reason she'd lasted where others had not.

She grounded him. She helped him square away his finances. Launder money. Invest it. He was a sail, she was a keel. And so they had passed through the years. It had been good and he hadn't thought much about it.

She didn't like what he did, and she never wanted to talk about it. She had never asked him to stop. Not with any force anyway. She had suggested, once, that things might have been different if they had had children. He refused to talk about such things, but he had never been able to get it out of his head.

Hobbs wondered what kind of father he would make. What was that job anyway? Raise a good citizen? He couldn't square that. Help a kid along his way? Maybe he could do that. But maybe not. Nobody had helped him, at least not any more than he'd helped them. Nobody except Grace.

And Alan? He was smart, could use computers. Why was he doing this? Hobbs knew. Not exactly why, but he knew that the kid had a hole in him, the kind that might never be filled. He wanted respect—all young men did—but beneath that he wanted freedom. He didn't want to live under somebody else's thumb—be a part of some corporate machine, work his way toward a shitty pension that they would jerk out from underneath him at the last minute.

Hobbs was old enough to know that some holes were just empty, sucking spaces that would never be filled. Someday he might be old enough to stop trying to fill his. But he doubted it. It would have happened by now.

FIFTEEN

Thirteen hours later Hobbs and Alan sat in a car that was parked on a cross street a block from Regent Armored. The windows were down and the early summer air, still hot from the day, blew through the compartment. It was just warm enough to be relaxing. It was the kind of breeze that brought with it images of sunburned children, exhausted from running and laughing, being tucked between clean white sheets by loving mothers with the promise that tomorrow would be exactly the same. That summer would never end. That school would never start again.

Like all good things, thought Hobbs, it was a lie. But what to say to this kid and how to put words to this feeling that overcame him? Hobbs shook his head, trying to rid himself of this strange wave of emotion. What the fuck, was he going through menopause?

There was nothing he could say to the kid. You can tell people only what they already know—especially in this rough trade. But maybe. Maybe. Then he realized what was bothering him.

"Gimme the gun," said Hobbs.

"What?" asked Alan, shocked and confused.

"I said gimme the gun. It's not going to help with what you have to do."

"What gun?" asked Alan, trying to sell it.

"I know you've got a piece. Young punks like you always do."

"Is this like that scene in *Star Wars*," he asked, "when Luke Skywalker goes into the cave on Dagobah, and Yoda tells him not to take the lightsaber with him?"

"*Star Wars*?" asked Hobbs.

"You know, the movie," Alan said.

"No, I don't."

"You've never seen *Star Wars*?"

"No," said Hobbs, not taking his eyes off Alan. Carefully noting the positions of his hands.

"OK, well, there's this Jedi master..."

"Kid."

"...and there's Luke, right, who's gonna be a badass later, but he's just learning—like I'm learning from you, right?" he said, laying it on a little thick.

"Kid."

"And never mind that he's like a million years old, almost as old as you—"

Hobbs slapped him across the face, hard. Alan looked back at him in shock. He clapped a hand to his cheek.

Perfectly calm, Hobbs asked, "You done?"

Alan nodded.

"This isn't a movie. Not any kind. You're not the good guy, or the bad guy. You're a guy who's going to steal a truck. They're the guys who are going to stop you. That's it. Now gimme the gun."

"What if I get in trouble?"

"If you get in trouble, the best thing to do is pretend that you are drunk and stumbled in looking for a place to piss. But you get caught with a piece, or worse, you pull it and use it, you're just fucked." Hobbs triggered the mic on his wrist. "We good?"

They both heard Hurlocker's drawl fill their earpieces: "Five by five."

"What does *five by five* mean?" asked Alan, stalling.

"Gimme the gun."

"N-n-n-no. I'm not giving up my piece. It makes me feel better."

Hobbs shook his head. "Listen, do what you want, but if you shoot anybody—if you fuck this up in any way—Hurlocker and I are going to disappear and you are on your own."

"Just like Casper the Friendly Ghost?"

"No," said Hobbs, "like Caspar the professional fucking thief."

Alan nodded. Then he got out of the car. He crossed the street, turned the corner, and was gone. Hobbs was suddenly very glad he didn't have any kids.

In the earpiece Hurlocker said, "You're clear to the door."

Hobbs hated that he couldn't see the action from where he was parked. He had a part to play, and it would work only if he appeared to come out of nowhere.

Hurlocker said, "Shit, boy, what are you doing? That's the wrong way. Ah, Christ, he's chickening out."

Alan rounded the corner and walked quickly back to the car. Hobbs thought about hitting the ignition and driving away. What else was there left to say? He'd failed the audition.

Alan opened the door and handed the pistol to Hobbs butt-first. "You're right."

Hobbs said, "I been doing this awhile."

"I'll be back with a truck."

"Wait," said Hobbs, "take this." He handed Alan a piece of lead wrapped in worn black leather. Hobbs pointed to his temple and the back of his head and the base of his skull. "Here, here, or here. Puts 'em right out."

Alan looked at the slapjack, and fear flickered across his face.

"Don't be too eager to use it."

Alan patted the slapjack against the heel of his hand. Then he turned and walked back into the night.

Hobbs said into the mic, "Don't tell anybody I said this, but I think that kid might just be all right."

Alan's voice came through the earpiece: "I won't say a word. Now shut the fuck up, I have to concentrate."

Hurlocker said, "Clear to the door."

Hobbs drummed on the steering wheel.

"Guy coming out for a smoke," said Hurlocker.

"Got him," answered Alan.

"Don't…," said Hurlocker. It was quickly followed by, "OK, door is clear, drag him insi—Shit. He left a guy unconscious on the sidewalk."

"It's not gonna take me long enough for him to wake up," said Alan.

"Don't get cocky, kid," snapped Hobbs.

"You sure you've never seen *Star Wars*?"

"Hunker down behind that truck, one of the techs is looking your way," Hurlocker snapped.

"Is this one good?"

"No, it just got dropped off today," said Hurlocker.

"What do we care, we're not driving it to spring break," said Alan. Hobbs sighed. In the radio Alan chuckled quietly and said, "I'm just fucking with you."

"Clear," said Hurlocker. There was silence on the radio for a moment, then Hurlocker said, "Hold."

"It's open space between me and the office."

"Hold," said Hurlocker. Then, "Move to the right side of the truck." Damn it, thought Hobbs. He knew they needed him in the chase car, but he couldn't stand not seeing what was going on. He started the car. It was early, but it wouldn't matter much one way or the other. Just a tiny lapse due to nerves. He didn't stop in his worrying to worry about why he had nerves.

SIXTEEN

Alan opened the door to the office and stepped in as calm as could be. Not thirty feet away, three guys were lowering a massively armored body onto a chassis. As it hung from the caged-in lift crane, two guys were hammering on a bolt and swearing while a third guy held the tons of armor and three-and-a-half-inch bulletproof glass in place with his fingertips.

Earlier, Hobbs had told Alan, "Don't try to be sneaky. Don't rush. When they aren't looking, walk calmly to where you are going like you belong there. Do all that and don't look at them, then they won't look at you."

He did it and nobody noticed. He was amazed it worked. He was feeling good about himself, the job and life. But when he closed the door, he realized the office wasn't empty. A man looked up from the desk on the far side of the room and said, "Who are you?" He was an older man, maybe sixty, with dignified gray hair, running to respectable, moneyed fat. He looked at Alan over the top of reading glasses. His hand, holding up a strip of adding machine tape, was frozen in place as he awaited a response.

"You're not supposed to be here," said Alan. In his ear Hurlocker said, "One coming out. He's gonna find Sleepy on the sidewalk. Best hurry it along."

"What do you mean, I'm not supposed to be here! I'm goddamned Regent! The king," he said, tapping the brass nameplate that had "McCaffery" spelled out on it in black letters. "I own this place. And if you work for me, I own you too. Now tell me what you need, son. Or back to work."

"They sent me in here to...," Alan said, very peacefully.

"OK," McCaffery said, getting annoyed. "For what? What's the matter with you? Out with it. Are you slow? Are you somebody's nephew or kid brother?"

"Yeah," said Alan, because it was true.

"OK, that's great. You'll excuse me, I don't have time for some weirdo kid." McCaffery dismissed him with a hand wave and went back to totaling figures.

Alan tried not to blush with anger. He fought back the hot tears. He hated that word, *weirdo*. Always had. The kids at school had teased him because he didn't have a dad. Because he was interested in computers. Teased him for a thousand petty things that one kid will tease another for. And the calculator made him mad too. Reading figures off the screen and pounding them into a calculator. How stupid. What a terrible way to use technology!

He didn't let any of his emotions show when he said, "I've got something for you."

"OK," said McCaffery, annoyed. "Give it to me and get out."

Alan walked over to the desk. He pulled the slapjack out and extended it toward McCaffery. McCaffery was busy squinting at the screen. "Just leave it on the desk there."

Alan hit him on the temple with the slapjack. McCaffery collapsed into the monitor and knocked it over. Calm and steady, Alan caught the monitor with one hand and kept it from falling.

McCaffery was slumped over the desk, semiconscious. The air escaped from his lungs with a strange, sighing moan. Alan thought about hitting him again. And then again. Then again. He realized he could do it. He could kill a man and get away with it, as easily as he had betrayed his clan in the Universe of Strife. Except this was real. This was power.

He realized he was holding his breath when Hurlocker said, as calmly as if he were reporting on the weather, "One man, headed toward the office."

Alan went to the lockbox. He punched in the code and grabbed the keys he needed. When he turned, a shadow was silhouetted in the frosted glass of the door. There was a knock. On cat's feet Alan dashed across the office to stand beside the door.

Another knock. Alan lifted the sap high. The door opened and whoever it was stuck his head in and said, "Sir?"

Alan hesitated. He could see the man's shaved head, his dark skin. Maybe Italian, maybe Latino. There was a smear of grease on his cheek. A mechanic. He smelled of soap and cigarettes. Alan was so close he could even see acne scars beneath the man's five o'clock shadow. Close enough to lean over and kiss him, and the man was completely unaware.

The man looked at Alan. Alan brought the slapjack down.

The guy fell forward into the office. Alan grabbed his arm and dragged him in completely. Had anybody seen that? The mechanic wasn't completely out. He moaned and tried to get to his feet. Alan sapped him again, wincing at the hollow sound that was made when leather and metal bounced off skull. The mechanic stopped moving.

Alan stepped over the unconscious man and walked out of the office. He hung a right and headed for the door to the parking lot. He walked quickly, but not in a hurry. He had to fight against the adrenaline surging through his body. But when he got to the door, he couldn't help himself. He looked over his shoulder.

The third-shift guys were all huddled around the guy from the sidewalk, trying to bring him around. One of them felt Alan's gaze, looked up, and saw him.

His eyes flicked back and forth between Alan and the guy lying unconscious on the shop floor. Then he shouted, "*Hey!*"

Alan ran through the door and into the night. He found the armored car he wanted easily enough and climbed in. As he started the beast, he heard Hurlocker say, "He's got the package, but kicked the hornets' nest."

Hobbs said, "Copy."

Why were they so quiet? How could they not be excited? He had gotten the truck! Alan looked out the side window and saw men running toward him. They looked angry. Alan waved to them and stomped on the gas.

As he smashed through the gate, he keyed the mic and yelled, "*Yeeeeeeeehaw!*" He sped off, as much as anyone can speed in a vehicle that is as heavy and unwieldy as an armored truck. As he made the first turn, Hobbs slid in behind him, doing little more than an idle and weaving erratically. He was playing the part of the drunken salesman on the way back to his hotel, just in case pursuit needed to be slowed. But there was no pursuit.

Alan took a left and then another left. Then a third left into an alley that led to the courtyard of the building across the street. Somewhere ahead of him was a loading bay door, but all he could see was the darkness. The bay door was open, but earlier that day they had covered the entrance with tarps. Alan accelerated; in this thing he felt OK driving through a brick wall.

A flashlight pulsed from the middle of the tarps, and Alan corrected course. As the tarps parted around the truck, he slammed on the brakes. The truck skidded, slammed down a short ramp, and lurched awkwardly to a stop in the basement of the abandoned factory across the street from Regent Armored.

"Whoooooooo," Alan yelled again, into the mic. On the other side of the glass he could see Hurlocker clawing his earpiece out of his head. Alan opened the door and jumped down.

"Whoooo!" he yelled, running toward Hurlocker. He was going in for what? A high five, a hug, a chest bump? Hurlocker turned, clipped Alan's legs out from underneath him, and slammed him to the floor, winding the kid. “I heard you the first time,” Hurlocker said.

Hobbs eased his car in through the tarps. Hurlocker walked over to the car, leaving Alan on the floor gasping for air.

Hobbs said, “Nobody. I think we’re clear.”

Hurlocker nodded, and they closed the rolling steel door and pulled the tarps down. They used the tarps to cover the car and the armored truck. Hurlocker walked past the kid saying, “C’mon, get up.”

Hobbs helped Alan off the floor.

SEVENTEEN

They descended to a subbasement they had set up with cots and provisions. The plan was to stay in the warehouse long enough to spray the truck, change the plates, and let the heat die down. Alan moved seamlessly from gloating over his "accomplishment" to bitching that he couldn't leave the building. Eventually he sulked in the corner with his laptop. Playing some game that was incomprehensible to Hobbs. Something about fighting off an alien invasion.

Hurlocker practiced card tricks and tried to get Hobbs to play gin. When that failed, he dealt himself hand after hand of solitaire. When Alan said, "It'd be faster to play that on a computer," Hurlocker looked at him as if he were a creature from another planet.

"It's supposed to take a while. That's the whole point."

Hobbs was self-contained and answered all Alan's pestering questions with grunts. Alan kept after him. "But did I do a good job?"

"Kid, just shut up and wait like the rest of us."

But a little while after that, Hobbs said, "You want to help me paint the truck?" Alan lifted his head from the carnage on the screen. Hobbs was sure he was going to tell him to fuck off like a surly teenager. But to Hobbs's surprise, the kid said yes.

While they worked with hand sanders, grinding off the clear coat, Hobbs explained what it took to put a good paint job on a car. A clean room, meticulous attention to detail, coat after coat after coat. "The quality of a finish is time. But we don't need quality, just disguise. And we don't have to take it down to the metal, we just need to scratch up the old finish to let the new paint stick. A real finish, the kind of fine work you'd like on your own car, takes days and specialized equipment. We don't have any of that and we don't care."

Alan listened and took pleasure in the task. He waited a long time, but as they were masking off the windows and the chrome, he couldn't hold it in any longer.

"So am I in? I mean, did I pass the audition?" He asked so nicely, he could have been a completely different person from the snot-nosed brat of the past few days.

"Yeah, you're in," said Hobbs. "Go easy, kid. You've got a lot to learn. All of it, in fact. And it will go better if you have just a little humility."

"But when you've got mad skills, like I do," Alan said. When Hobbs looked over at him, he could see Alan was joking.

Hobbs smiled and said, "That was pretty slick with the security cameras."

"Yeah, I got lucky," said Alan, stripping a long piece of blue painter's tape from the roll. "Real cheeseball security. But it was pretty fucking cool, you gotta admit. I thought for sure you'd be impressed, but..."

"Tricks with computers are one thing," said Hobbs. "Everybody is brave at a distance, but in the middle of it, when the shit all goes wrong, that's when you figure out what somebody is made of."

"Yeah, that's why..."

"Why what?"

"Nah, man, you'll think I'm silly."

"We gotta lotta time to kill."

"OK, OK, it's like. So when you were my age, right? You know, back in the Stone Age, right? You know, wearing a leopard skin and draggin' a club around with some Barney Rubble–lookin' motherfucker."

"I'm not that old."

"But you're old enough that you've seen the world go to hell. It's helmets, right. Everything safe, everybody plays by the rules. So my uncle, right, he's the man. I mean in Philly, he's the man. All mobbed up, everybody gives him respect.

"My dad got clipped when I was young, and he stepped in and took care of my mom and me. Which I'm grateful for, you know, absolutely. But I'm a grown man. I don't need protecting anymore. I don't need the training wheels. I don't need the helmet. I gotta go out and do for *me*. Sure I'm gonna fall down and get fucked up, but I mean, how am I supposed to be a *man* if I don't do that?"

Hobbs nodded. "Yeah, that's the way it works."

"There's something wrong with me, Caspar, and I know it. I am the most comfortable motherfucker you have ever met in your life. People have been giving me everything I've ever wanted my whole life. And none of it means a thing. People respect me because of who my uncle is. I get mad respect, everywhere I go. But inside, I don't even respect myself."

Hobbs nodded, not working on the truck anymore.

"That's why I want to do this. So I can hold my head up and know it's not just some bullshit I'm throwing to impress some girl. Or to hide how scared I am."

"Nobody can give you self-respect," said Hobbs.

"Naw, man, you gotta take it."

"Steal it," said Hobbs.

"Can you help me? Can you help me do that?"

Hobbs looked at him for a long time, saying nothing. Alan didn't look away.

"If you listen, I can help you," said Hobbs.

"But you will. You'll help me figure out how to steal *that*?"

Hobbs nodded. "Now let's get this thing sprayed." He changed the pressure setting on the compressor and hooked up two spray guns.

"Don't we need masks?"

"You're young, you'll heal. And I'm so old I don't think it makes a difference anymore." When Hobbs saw the face that Alan was making, he laughed. "What, you want to live forever?"

"Yeah, don't you?"

"I'll skip the shitting-in-a-bag years at the end, if you don't mind." He clipped a wire to the undercarriage of the armored truck. "This runs a current, a negative charge through the truck." He held up the sprayer. "Positive charge, so the paint is magnetically attracted to the truck."

"Doesn't that blow a fuse or something? It would wreck a computer."

"It's not much, but even if it was, this whole thing is what they call a Faraday cage. It's why you can be in a car that's hit by lightning and you and the car will be fine. Charge stays on the skin. Rubber tires keep it insulated, no problem."

"Huh."

"Yeah, it would be easier for us if it didn't work that way. Just cram a Taser into the side and knock out all the people and the GPS tracker and the radios. But it doesn't work that way."

"But then how are you going to knock out the tracker?"

"I'm going to do it with style. Now c'mon, we gotta get this thing painted, you don't have to learn everything in a day."

They sprayed the truck down. It was still tacky when Hobbs set out that night for Panama City, Florida. Hobbs had planned on making the drive by himself, but he asked the kid to ride shotgun.

Hurlocker split off to pick up a few more things and said that he would meet them in a week. As he said good-bye to Hobbs he asked, "Is there anything more beautiful than the love between an older man and a young boy?"

"Fuck you."

Hurlocker, serious, said, "Watch yourself."

EIGHTEEN

Three hours into the drive, Hobbs gave Alan the gun back. He asked him, "You know what kind of gun it is?"

Alan shook his head.

"Charter Arms Bulldog, .44 Special. Good gun to hit somebody with. Doesn't shoot so good. Where'd you get it?"

"My uncle."

"You know what he did with it? Before you got it?"

"Left it in my mother's bedroom."

Hobbs drove for a while, saying nothing. Then he said, "So he could have killed some guy with it. You get caught with it, that's on you."

"My uncle isn't the kind of guy who kills people."

"You think he's a nice guy or something?"

"No, I know he's a bad man. But he's the kind of guy who hires somebody else to do it. At least now he is."

Hobbs nodded, taking in a new fact. Then he said, "Next bridge we come to, you throw that out the window and into the water. We already got all the hardware we need for this job."

"But it's my gun."

"I never met your uncle, but I can tell you something about him right now. He's got a small dick."

"I wouldn't know anything about that," said Alan, impassively looking out the window into the night. "But my mom would."

"I feel sorry for your mom."

"Don't feel sorry for my mother," Alan said. "She deserves what she gets."

"What she's gettin' ain't much," Hobbs said. That one got to Alan. Hobbs saw the hurt and anger flash across Alan's face. Hobbs said, "That gun is almost the right idea, small, reliable, but unless you are going to mug an elk, nobody needs that much gun. Thirty-eight is plenty if you know how to shoot. But shooting is almost always a mistake. You shouldn't need to use a gun at all if you do everything right."

"Have you ever needed to use a gun?"

"They scare civilians. Mostly I've just hit people with them."

"Have you ever shot anybody?"

Hobbs took a while before he answered, "Only people who tried to cross me."

"How many of them are there?"

"Were," said Hobbs. "How many of them *were* there."

They drove over six bridges, big and small, before they got to where they were going. Alan kept the gun in his pocket. As they went over one of the bridges, Alan asked, "How do I know *you're* not gonna cross *me*?"

Hobbs smiled and said, "You don't."

And that was the last they spoke of the gun.

PART THREE
FROM VICTORY, DEFEAT

ONE

Five minutes before

Five weeks later Hobbs and Alan sat in a pickup truck with magnetic signs on the door panels that read, "Johnson Civil Surveyors." The truck was parked atop a small hill, looking down on an empty bridge, forty-five minutes south of Tallahassee on US Route 319. Ten feet in front of the truck a pole was stuck in the ground, the kind that surveyors would sight with theodolite.

The bridge was a little over a half a mile long, and had recently been rebuilt because the powers that be had seen fit to dredge out this swampy tributary of the Ochlockonee River in order to make it, of all things, more accessible for fishermen.

There was not a fisherman in sight. And all the times that they had been here, scouting, setting up, rehearsing, and covering their tracks, neither Hobbs nor Hurlocker nor Alan had even seen a boat, much less a fisherman. But Florida had a long tradition of not being able to leave natural waterways alone. That, and spending matching federal funds to generate as much kickback as possible.

Ten minutes before, they had blocked off this end of the bridge with a barrier and a sign that read, "Bridge Repair, Temporary Delay." On the other side of the bridge, Hurlocker was waiting with a similar sign, around the bend. When the armored truck passed, he would close the bridge from that end. As long as the truck was alone, the plan would work. But last Wednesday—it was always a Wednesday, for payday was always a Friday—a sad-faced old woman had been tailgating the truck and they hadn't been able to peel her off. So they had scrubbed it for a week.

Hobbs had thought they would never hear the end of it from Hurlocker. "What kind of moon-faced, gas-huffing, inbred, white-trash, roadkill-poachin'—?"

"Redneck," offered Alan with a shrug.

"Don't you talk about my people that way!" Hurlocker had bellowed, needing to vent his anger no matter the logic or reason.

"Easy," said Hobbs. But that just inflamed Hurlocker all the more. He had stomped out of the house and wandered off to the beach, there to vent his fury on the indifferent waves and the impossible-to-catch ghost crabs.

Alan had looked at Hobbs and smiled. Hobbs, for once, smiled back. They sat on the porch of the house, an old cinder-block beach bungalow, built in a time before only rich people could afford houses on the coast.

After a while Alan broke the silence with, "It's the waiting, isn't it? The waiting is what makes or breaks you." And that's when Hobbs knew he finally understood.

"He's steady enough," Hobbs said, nodding after Hurlocker. "He's just throwing a fit because he doesn't have anything better to do. He's bored."

"He shouldn't make so much fun of computer games, then," said Alan.

In the past weeks, Alan had really come along. He had calmed down and stopped being so much of a punk. He listened. He asked questions that weren't stupid. He'd learned to scuba dive and work a cutting torch.

Over the years Hobbs had seen a lot of guys leave the straight world behind. It wasn't an easy transition. With most of them, you could tell right away they wouldn't make it. The heavy heist was a rough trade, and perhaps a dying game as well. It was harder and harder to get away with. Fucking cameras and fucking computers dragging the world closer and closer together. Cops dressed like storm troopers now and were armed to the teeth.

Hobbs was a bad man, sure, but even he saw something wrong with this. The balance had tipped too far in favor of authority, and it was harder and harder for a red-blooded man to make any move on his own. Everybody was on the fear ladder. The cops, the criminals. Everybody answered to another higher-up all the way up the line, until you got to the rarefied air at the top of the org chart that was too thin for any kind of responsibility to survive.

Hobbs hadn't been born with wealth, but he didn't want to live his life knuckling under for anyone. If it took courage and discipline and violence to tear a life for himself out of society, well, fine. He'd paid the cost, and he'd go on paying—as long and as much as it took to stay free.

As much as it surprised him, the kid gave him hope. He hadn't seen anybody like this come along in a while. Maybe it was that the times were too soft. The lure of an easy job was seductive. After all, if you had intelligence and discipline, why not go domestic? Sell out. Suck the corporate teat. Mostly the stupid and the broken turned to crime. Didn't take long before those kinds went to jail. For them prison had a revolving door.

But Alan was different. He was *smart*. He understood computers and how to make them work for him. Maybe the heist wasn't a dying game. Maybe it was just that the times had passed Hobbs by. Sure, a job would always call for a strong arm and a steady mind, but maybe that wasn't enough anymore.

They sat in the truck and watched the bridge through thick, sweltering air. They ran the engine so the air-conditioning would blow cool. If they had done this job twenty-five years ago, they'd both be sitting in pools of sweat right now.

Shitty music blared from Alan's earbuds, and he bopped along in time with the endless drone of the trancelike electronic music. The kid kept the strange time of the music by beating his thumbs on the steering wheel.

For the thousandth time today, Hobbs sighted between the two carefully placed vertical strips of painter's tape on the windshield. He checked the radar gun on a passing seagull. It was flying at thirteen miles an hour.

On the open glove compartment lid the LED on the remote trigger still glowed green, showing a good connection with the device. In all the time they had sat there, that light hadn't flickered even once. It shouldn't have, given what they had paid for it. And each of the three weeks they had tried to take the truck, Hobbs had cleaned all the connections and replaced all the batteries before every attempt.

Once they had set up the job, they'd had little else to do but wait. He and Hurlocker had tried to teach the kid poker, but it didn't take. Alan had made a ritual out of making fun of how early Hobbs got up to run and do push-ups. Three days ago Alan had tried to keep up with Hobbs and failed miserably. The teasing had stopped after that. Sometimes the weight of Hobbs's years was something he could bludgeon somebody with.

Hobbs sighted through the strips and checked the gun again. The bridge wasn't moving, at zero miles per hour.

The song pumping through Alan's earbuds changed, and Hobbs frowned, deep lines cutting deeper into his face. It was loud enough that he could hear the inane lyrics repeated over and over again.

"Turn down for what? Whatever. Just turn it the fuck down already." But he knew he was just cranky from waiting. He got grumpy the same way the kid cranked up his music and drummed the steering wheel. Still, being grumpy was something to do.

"You should turn it down," Hobbs said.

Alan looked over at him with a quizzical look on his face. He hooked a finger and yanked the earbud out of his right ear. "Huh?" he asked.

"Nothing," said Hobbs.

Alan gave a nod that was all upward jerk and screwed the bud back in tight. *He should be paying more attention*, thought Hobbs. *He should be more patient.* That was just more nerves. Hobbs was patient enough for the both of them.

The radio crackled to life. Hurlocker's voice from the ether. "Coming, in the clear."

Beside him Alan popped both earbuds out of his head with a sharp jerk. "Is this it? I mean, is it going to happen this time?"

"Steady," said Hobbs, to both the kid and himself. "Forty seconds, maybe less." Hobbs picked up the remote trigger. He flipped the safety off, thinking of all those Cold War scenes he'd seen in movies where they flipped the fail-safe off. His thumb hovered over the switch. The LED on the side still glowed green.

"C'mon. C'mon," Alan muttered. The shitty music squealed through the earbuds. Hobbs wanted to tell him to turn it off, but he didn't want to lose focus. Still, that music was so terrible.

It was a good play. If it came off, there'd be no snatch, no getaway, no chance of a gunfight. Just more waiting. The waiting could be harder on the nerves than action, but it was safer.

"There it is."

On the other side of the river, they saw the Moonis-Brainerd truck round the long curve toward the bridge footing. On the far side of the road the swamp gave way to a lake filled with white lily pads and their blossoms. The lake, such as it was, emptied into the channel and flowed under the bridge as if it had all the time in the world, which it did.

Hobbs hit the truck with the radar gun. Fifty-three miles an hour. They were taking their time today. Sixty miles an hour would be a tenth of a mile every six seconds. They were slower,

Hobbs would just have to feel it. Shouldn't matter much. Hobbs sighted between the two pieces of tape on the windshield until the surveyor's pole appeared like the front sight on a rifle between them.

"One Miss-is-sippi, Two Miss—is-sippi," Hobbs said deliberately.

"C'mon," said Alan, "Do it!"

"Three Miss-is-sippi. Four Miss—"

Hobbs pressed the button. Alan held his breath.

TWO

"Yeah, but the thing is, with a sailboat, you can go anywhere. I mean anywhere you want. Just think about it."

"Put your seat belt on, Ray. It's company policy."

"What are you? An old woman? You want me to wear a helmet too?"

"Ray..."

"I'll put my seat belt on if you just think about it."

"Think about it? You are trapped inside this armored can with me every working day, endless fucking miles in this truck, and you tell me that when you retire, you want to trade this small room in for another one? You just don't make no kinda sense, Ray."

Ray looked out through the thick bulletproof-glass windshield and gestured to the glorious sky and verdant wetlands sliding by on either side of the truck. "But all this beauty. With no place to be, the wind on your face."

"The rain," said Pete, his hands resting lightly on the wheel. "You do realize it rains out there? And then you're trapped in a little wooden box, probably at sea in the middle of a storm. You're gonna drown, Ray. They won't even let you drive the truck, and you think you can captain a boat?"

Ray was undaunted. "I don't need anybody to clear me to drive my own boat. And they won't clear me because they don't want to have to pay me a dollar fifty an hour more."

Pete knew the reason they wouldn't clear him was that they had found out he had had a DUI a ways back. Now they wouldn't even have hired him, but as he had been an otherwise good employee, they had grandfathered him in. Pete kept his mouth shut because he didn't want to have to hear Ray whine about it for the next ten thousand miles they rode together. Fucking guy talked too much as it was.

"But all the fresh air and the beautiful views," Ray droned on.

"Fresh air? Lemme ask you a question. You're all battened down—that's what they call it, right—all your hatches are battened down for the night. And the wind and the rain are howling outside, right? Where do you go to the bathroom?"

"Well, the boat has a toilet."

"You mean like a regular crapper?"

"They call it a head," Ray said, proud of himself for using a nautical term, "a marine toilet."

"It's a port-a-potty. A chemical toilet. It's *worse* than riding in this truck. Not only are you going to be trapped in a small box, you're gonna be trapped in a small box with a pot of your own shit and piss. Ray, that ain't retirement. That's my idea of hell."

"But the fresh sea air...," Ray added weakly. Trailing off into silence and whatever thoughts he could muster.

Pete was grateful to hear the rumble of the engine and the roar of the run-flat tires for a change. The wind cried a little around the corners of the cab as the brutishly nonaerodynamic armored truck hammered through it. There wasn't a curve to be found on these things. And in all the time he had been driving these beasts, there never had been. It was as if some designer somewhere had said, "Make 'em angry and square. People just won't think they're safe if they ain't square."

In the silence Pete almost found himself enjoying the view. But it was no good. He had driven it too many times. Inside the air-conditioning it seemed beautiful. But he knew it was like walking into a moist cotton diaper. Full of alligators and mosquitos and not much else. For some goddamned reason, this is where Ponce de León had thought the Fountain of Youth was. Traipsed all over this godforsaken swamp looking for it. They even had a town farther back named for it. Panacea—cure-all. This swamp was cure for nothing, except maybe health and excitement.

As he passed a surveyor standing next to his truck in the heat he felt grateful that he didn't have that poor bastard's job. Jesus Christ, standing around in that heat, measuring things that nobody cared about. He wondered how many times they had to run away from alligators in ditches, or water moccasins. Or how many of them had been killed by falling asleep at the wheel in the middle of all this emptiness and running off the road.

It had to have happened. It seemed as if those surveyors were always out here. For the last month or so, he had passed those guys and their sticks and tripods. Probably some make-work contract awarded by the state. The man who owned the company sending his guys out to sweat and taking a fat markup off it. Using some of that cash to buy drinks and hookers for some committee man or minor official who had awarded the job in the first place. Pete knew how the world worked. There was a club. He wasn't in it.

What would they get out of a survey anyway? "Yeah, Bob, it's swampy and nasty. Once again, we've confirmed that you don't want to build anything here." Pete snickered a little, and the sound brought Ray back to life.

"What's so funny?"

"Nothing."

"No, really, Ray, what is it?"

"Put your seat belt on."

They came around a bend, and ahead of them he saw the bridge, as straight and narrow as the barrel of a rifle. Pete wondered if, if he drove it fast enough, he'd be able to launch himself out of this shitty job for good. But as the truck eased up on the bridge, he kept her speed steady. They had trackers on these trucks. Sure, to protect the money, but also to chap his ass if he went too fast or too slow. They said it was for fuel economy, but Pete thought it was just so the bean crunchers could have another thing to chap his ass about.

There was a violent bump. Then the truck left the pavement. Ray sawed at the wheel, but nothing happened. The engine raced. He saw blue sky through the window as the weight of the rear armored compartment pulled the truck down ass-first.

There was a jolt as the rear of the truck hit the ground. The front wheels slammed toward the earth, and everything was thrown violently around the cab. Pete bounced off the steering wheel and heard a cracking sound.

He felt the vehicle list backward and to the right. Then he saw the water bubble up around the edge of the windshield. They hadn't hit the ground. They were in the river! The engine coughed, sucked water, and drowned.

Pete hit the panic button on the side of the steering column again and again, but nothing happened. All the electronics were dead.

"Ray? Ray!" Pete said. As if in answer, Ray slumped over on him. "Get off of me," Pete snapped, not realizing his co-driver was dead. As the water rose higher and higher on the windshield, Pete fought against the panic. He heard the water gurgling in through the vents, filling the compartment.

Not even anchors sank this fast.

The truck hit bottom, settling on its tires, and Ray's body tumbled off the side window and splashed into Pete. "Jesus, Ray!" Then he realized Ray was dead.

Thrashing wildly, on the ragged edge of losing it, Pete pushed Ray's corpse away from him. The water was up to Pete's chest.

He chanted, "Could be worse, could be worse, could be worse." Worst mantra ever.

Pete waited until the water was all the way up to the ceiling before he tried to open the heavily armored door. But it wouldn't budge. He took another breath in the rapidly dwindling air space, then tried again. Nothing. He tried the other door, but it wouldn't open. He went up for air and there was nothing.

He died fighting to get the passenger side door open.

THREE

"Whooooooooo!" In the seat next to Hobbs, Alan beat on the steering wheel in triumph. "Goooooooooooooo-oooooooooal!"

"Enough," said Hobbs, but happiness leaked through his gruff demeanor. Alan threw the door open and ran around outside the car yelling, "—oooooooooooooooooooooooooal!" like an Argentinian who'd just scored in the final of the World Cup.

"Get back in the car, you jackass," Hobbs called, laughing, "unless you want me to drive."

"Aw, come on," he said from the other side of Hobbs's window. "Did you see that? It was like a movie, man. Like a movie. Better than a movie. In a movie the bad guys don't get away with it."

"We haven't gotten away with it yet," said Hobbs grimly. It was the hard-won knowledge of a career that had lasted longer than this kid had been alive—there were a million ways a job could go wrong and only one it could go right. Just a matter of the odds. Still, he had to smile at the kid's euphoria. It had been a thing of beauty.

When Hobbs had pressed the button, two high-pressure ram jacks had lifted a piece of the metal bridge decking. The left side had risen a full eight inches higher than the right. The result was that the surface of the road had, almost instantly, become a ramp. As the fifty-five-thousand-pound truck hit it at fifty-three miles per hour, it was lifted sharply into the air and drifted over the guardrail. It seemed impossible that something that heavy could fly that far, but fly it had. Nearly thirty feet out into the center of the freshly dredged channel, before it hit the water.

The rear bumper splashed first, and then the front end of the cab. The sudden upward shock of the ramp and then the whipping action of the cab hitting the water caused Hobbs to wonder if the guys inside had been wearing their seat belts. Would be better for them if they hadn't, he thought grimly.

Hobbs didn't like killing people. His dislike wasn't unprofessional, because killing people just brought more heat. But this was the cleanest way, the only way, he could figure how to do the job. Hobbs didn't waste time feeling sorry for himself. He couldn't see why he should feel sorry for somebody else.

As he watched $23 million sink into the murky water of the Ochlockonee River, Hobbs said, "And for my next trick..."

It was all hell getting the kid to drive slowly back to the house.

FOUR

And then, more waiting.

All good heists are magic tricks. You take a thing in such a way that the audience doesn't know where it was taken and doesn't even know how to find it. Misdirection for ill-gotten gain.

Everybody professional knows that the best way to make a getaway is not to get away at all, but to stay put until the search radius has spread out, then leave slowly and quietly. You don't have to get ahead of the pursuit when it's far in front of you, or it's been called off.

But what Hobbs had just pulled off was even better. It really was stealing something without taking it. For the rest of it, they'd just be three guys on a fishing trip. All but impossible to prove otherwise. They'd let all that money soak, and when the soak was done, they would pull it up from the bottom of the channel and drive away like any other right citizen, but with a trunkful of damp cash.

Sure, none of the three of them was going to let either of the others out of his sight until the split, because there was always that danger of somebody going for the cross on any job. But this one was safer. Fewer people. And it wasn't as if there were a ready bag of cash anybody could grab and go. They had to dredge it up.

Nope, nothing to do for at least a week but fish and tell each other lies.

That night they built a fire in the sand and roasted oysters on a steel plate. They scattered them with a shovel and then covered them with a beer-soaked towel. As soon as the oysters popped open, they scooped them into the bed of one of the trucks, cracked them with screwdrivers, and sucked them down. The fresh, sharp tang of the sea, mixed with the beer, tasted like victory.

When they had eaten their fill, Hurlocker said, "I don't know about you boys, but I'm goin' to bed. We gotta lotta fishin' to do this next week. I need to save my strength."

He went back to the house and left Hobbs and Alan out underneath the stars beside a dying fire. To Hobbs's surprise, the kid was quiet and didn't ruin the moment with some pointless chatter, or shitty music pouring forth from earbuds.

They looked up at the sky for a long, long time before Alan asked, "Is that the Milky Way?"

"Yeah," said Hobbs.

Alan pitched his empty beer can into the back of the truck. Then he looked out at the ocean. Far, far out to sea were three flashes of lightning. There was no sound. Alan said, "You know, I don't know how to fish."

"You've got nothing to do for the next week but learn."

Alan smiled at him and said, "I've got nothing to do. I mean nothing."

Hobbs thought of Grace and it pinched his heart sharply. He tried not to think of her while he was working. Jobs usually didn't go on long enough for him to miss her. For a foolish instant, he wished she were there on that beach with him. He would take her in his arms, kiss her, and tell her what she wanted to hear more than anything in the world. That this was the last one. That he was done. That she would get what she wanted and never have to worry about him again.

He'd pause after that. She would be crying, softly. Then he would wipe away a tear and say, "Be careful what you wish for." And he would tell her all this even though he would be sure it was a lie. Because, even though he rarely admitted it, even to himself, he loved her, and the words would make her happy. There, on the beach, under the stars, with storms far off in the distance, next to a dying fire, it would be a perfect moment. And even though he was a thief, he would not dream of robbing her of that.

"How many guys do you think were in the truck?" Alan asked.

"Does it matter?"

"It's just, I never killed anybody before."

"And you still haven't. I pushed the button. It's on me," Hobbs said.

"I helped you set it up. I carried gear, ran hydraulic tubes, I helped."

"If you loaded a gun for me and I shot somebody with it, would that be your fault?"

"No, but..."

"Kid, forget it. It's done and there's no undoing it."

"What are you going to do, huh? I mean after," Alan said, either ruining the moment or bringing Hobbs back to his senses.

"I dunno, kid. Ask me when it's over."

"But it's over. I mean, we did it, right? We got away with it."

Hobbs shook his head. "Not until we've got the cash and get away clean. Not until it's laundered. There's a thousand kindsa things that can go wrong with a job. Probably a thousand and one. But I've seen a thousand. We had a good day, that's it."

"I got a good feelin', though," said Alan.

"That's when it all goes sideways, kid. You just stay calm, don't do anything stupid, and take it like it comes."

FIVE

They spent the next two days fishing, not catching much of anything, and not minding in the slightest. The tropical storms remained visible in the south, but they stayed there. They could see flashes of lightning even during the day, but above them the skies were clear. They were up before the sun and in bed before the moon rose. Sunburned and happy, they grew forty-eight hours older.

On the third day, Hobbs woke up to the sound of a mechanical voice reading a hurricane warning. Hurlocker looked up from the weather radio and said, "Sounds like the ocean is closed."

Hobbs rubbed his eyes and poured himself a cup of coffee. They let the kid sleep and the radio cycle through its prerecorded message. Neither of them said anything. They just took turns refilling their coffee and looking at a map of the Gulf of Mexico that hung on the wall.

When the dawn came, it was ugly and wet. No yellow or red in it at all, just lighter and lighter black visible through the rain-spattered windows. The wind picked up and they heard the surf pounding the Gulf side of the point.

By the time Alan woke, the mechanical voice on the radio was talking about "mandatory evacuations." Hurricane Kristy was expected to make landfall as a category three sometime late that night or the next day. Alan rubbed the sleep from his eyes and headed straight to his laptop.

Hurlocker said, "We outstayed Mother Nature's welcome."

Hobbs said, "She's a bitch, anyway," as he looked out the windows toward the pounding of the ocean.

"This thing is a monster," said Alan. On his screen he had weather maps and forecasts. Over the last forty-eight hours the storm had turned nearly ninety degrees and accelerated rapidly to the north. All the projections for the path of the hurricane came right through them. Like the wrath of God, headed straight for them.

Hurlocker looked at the screen and said, "That's the kind of thing that gives beachfront property a bad name."

"One thousand and one," said Hobbs.

"What?" asked Hurlocker.

"Ways a job can go wrong."

Alan looked at Hobbs and asked, "What do we do?"

Hurlocker said, "No offense, gentlemen, but I don't trust either of y'all fine motherfuckers enough to let y'all outta my sight until this thing is done." Then he laughed, but the laugh had teeth in it.

Hobbs nodded and stared at the weather animation. A screen filled with green and red, clawing their way out of the Gulf of Mexico. "There's no way they've called off the search for that truck already. But a hurricane…" Hobbs rubbed his left cheek with his right hand.

"We go get it. Right now, get it and get out of here," said Alan.

Hobbs shook his head. "Patience. We wait. The way to do it is wait until everybody is gone, wait until the leading edge of the storm hits, and then grab it."

Alan said, "But it's a fucking hurricane!"

Hurlocker and Hobbs both gave Alan a flat look.

Finally Hurlocker said, "You gonna melt if you get wet, kid?"

"It just seems, I dunno, risky."

Hurlocker burst into laughter, doubling over in amusement. Even Hobbs couldn't keep from chuckling. Especially when Alan looked hurt. When he couldn't get a word in through the wilderness of Hurlocker's laughter, he pouted.

"Shit, son," Hurlocker said, struggling to regain his breath, "that's what we do. We take chances and hope they pay off."

Hobbs said, "We'll be underwater for the worst of it. Then put the cash in the dive bags, layer of gear on top, then we're just evacuating like anybody else. If it doesn't hit hard, we'll be fine. If it does hit hard, that's more cover and distraction for us."

Hobbs looked at Hurlocker, who was nodding in approval. Hobbs said, "Hurt, we're gonna need a chain saw. There's no way we're getting out of here in a boat. Anything we can't drive over, we're gonna have to hack through."

"Walmart is about twenty minutes inland."

"No, there has to be one somewhere on this island. Wait till most everybody clears out, then go shed to shed."

"It's an isthmus," said Alan.

"What?" said Hobbs.

"We're not on an island," Alan mumbled. "It's attached to the land. It's an isthmus."

Hurlocker tapped Alan's computer screen. "Son, in about twelve hours, this is gonna be an island, one way or another. Maybe even a reef."

Hobbs said, "We'll stage a truck up at the bridge. We'll try to take the boat upriver; if not, we'll drive and work from the land."

"So what can I do?" asked Alan.

"Right now? You're gonna wait," said Hobbs.

Alan frowned. "I don't like it. I don't like the waiting. I don't like any of it."

The last hint of a smile fell from Hobbs's face, and he said, "You have a better chance we can take?"

Alan shook his head.

"OK," said Hobbs.

They pulled the trucks around the back of the house so that they were no longer visible, then sat on the screened-in porch with the lights off and watched the residents of Alligator Point, Florida, pack up and leave.

That night, under the cover of a driving rain, they drove back to the bridge and hid one of the trucks by the bridge footing.

By four in the afternoon the next day, the rain and the wind had driven them inside. The waves on the beach sounded like shelling, and the scrub pines and scraggly palms outside the windows were often bent horizontal by the wind.

Hobbs smiled wide like a hungry wolf and said, "Ladies, they're playing our song. Let's load the boat."

Hobbs had his coat on and was outside before either of them could say anything. Alan said, "The worse things get, the happier he is."

"Yeah," said Hurlocker, as if it had been a ridiculous thing to say. Then he slapped Alan on the ass and said, "Giddyap, mule!"

Most of the dive gear was on the boat already. What took the most time was clearing the house. Hurlocker mixed a bottle of bleach and water and used it to spray and wipe everything they had touched. Then he poured straight bleach into all the drains. "Don't want any DNA tests," he said.

Alan asked, "Won't they know there was bleach? Isn't that suspicious?"

"Oxidant," said Hurlocker, drawling it out to four syllables. "If anybody thinks to look here, it will just be whatever it is combined with oxygen. And oxygen ain't suspicious in the slightest. 'Less you want to say it causes global warming."

Alan shouldered the last load from the house and carried it outside. The rain came down in sheets and it was hard to see the stairs in the dark. Out by the dock was a high-powered streetlight on a pole. Alan headed for it. Directly beneath it Hobbs had a tank of air and the scuba rigs. He was checking them.

Alan said as he passed, "You're gonna get all wet out here."

"Better than getting all drowned," Hobbs snapped. "Bring me that tool kit from below."

When Alan came back up from belowdecks, Hobbs and Hurlocker were hunched over a regulator, faces wrinkled with concern. Alan dropped the toolbox in the sand.

Hurlocker said, "Well, fuck you, then. He can hold the flashlight."

Hobbs shook his head in disgust as Hurlocker splashed off toward the boat.

Then, from the darkness, a voice yelled, "Freeze, FBI!"

SIX

Hobbs turned his head toward the voice, but he could see nothing but the streaks of raindrops burned white by the light above. Hopeless. Still, he thought about diving to the side and pulling his gun.

Hurlocker had frozen in midstep. Hobbs had heard him rail about the "federals" enough to know that he would never be taken alive. *Fine*, thought Hobbs. *If this is it, then this is it.* Then he looked at the kid.

It was a mistake. He saw Alan making the same slow-motion mistake. Thinking too much. But worse than that, he was just a kid. He had his whole life in front of him. And he was going to go for a hopeless pull on assailants in the dark. Hobbs couldn't move. Wet and shivering and old and exhausted, something came back to him. He couldn't have the kid throw all his tomorrows away for…for him, for money, for nothing.

He opened his mouth to tell him to stop. The kid hadn't made his move yet, but Hobbs could see it coming. He was too slow. Too late. His lips parted, his diaphragm contracted. The hiss of the beginning of the *s* in the word *stop* slid from his lips. And then there was the roar of gunfire.

Something knocked him off his feet. He went down and gasped for a breath that wouldn't come. There was no pain. And that scared him even more. He was on the ground and he couldn't get up. He felt warm urine running down his leg and ignored the shame of it as if it had come from someone else.

Hurlocker was sprawled in the sand, facing away from him. He wasn't moving. Hobbs was sure he was dead. On the ground, maybe ten feet from Hurlocker, Alan kicked and screamed, clutching his right thigh.

Hobbs tried to speak. Tried to tell him. Tried to curse God and fate and the voice in the darkness, but in his chest was only pain.

A man in an FBI windbreaker emerged from the darkness. He said, "What in the hell did you do that for?" Angry, surprised, sounding off balance and out of control. He did not look away as he spoke, only cycled his gaze and his gun through the three men lying on the ground.

A blond woman entered the pool of illumination beneath the tungsten light. Her short hair was plastered to her head by the rain. It made her look like a beautiful skull.

"I said what the fuck!" said the man.

She walked past the man in the windbreaker and knelt next to Alan. She frisked him and found his gun. "Check the others," she said, all business.

"How about fuck you! I'm not doing shit until you tell me why you just went all Rambo."

"Is that a weapon?" she asked, pointing at Hurlocker's corpse.

The man shifted his gaze. Even racked by pain and trying to catch his breath, Hobbs saw it coming. Hell, it was even funny. The nudnik looking away, the woman raising Alan's gun and shooting him through the back of the skull. The man's body falling heavily on the wet, sandy soil.

Seeing this, Hobbs wanted to laugh one last bitter laugh before he died, but he could not. His chest convulsed once and there was a flash of white. For a moment he saw nothing but pain.

When he opened his eyes again, the woman was standing over Alan. She asked, "Where's the money?"

Alan said something, but his words were drowned out by the rain and the roar of blood in Hobbs's ears.

She stepped on the kid's leg and Alan screamed. Then, in the exact same tone of voice, she asked again, "Where's the money?"

This time Hobbs heard Alan say, "Fuck you."

She shot him in the other leg.

The cold, professional part of Hobbs knew what was going to happen, what *had* to happen to all of them. Maybe there would be more or less suffering, but the end would be the same. But still, stupid as it was, he was proud of that "Fuck you."

The woman stood on both of Alan's legs now and his scream rose to a peak and disappeared. There was the roar of thunder and another flash. Hobbs thought she had shot him again, but no. It was just the storm.

"OK, OK, it's still in the truck," Alan screamed. This was enough to buy him a temporary reprieve. She got off his leg.

"Where's the truck?" the woman asked, sounding almost bored with the whole thing.

Alan told her, quite simply, where the truck was. He even added latitude and longitude. Kid was smart. He liked that play even better than the "Fuck you."

The woman said, "Thank you," with exaggerated politeness. Then she shot him in the head.

Even though there was no point to it, even though it was inefficient and unprofessional, Hobbs tried to cry out. He tried to get up. To do something. To hurl himself in rage at this woman from the storm. He tried. But he couldn't. So he fell back in the mud and tried to die.

SEVEN

Hobbs woke up when his head slammed into the deck of the boat. The woman had dragged him to the dock and rolled him in. He could see what was left of Hurlocker next to him. The blackness danced around the edges of his eyes and he tried to pull it together. His limbs felt cold and sluggish. How could he not be dead? He had given up.

Alan's corpse landed on top of him. He heard footsteps on the deck, then the engine starting beneath him. There was a lurch as the boat was put in gear and headed out into the canal. What was she doing?

As the boat sped up, he struggled to get Alan's corpse off him. Through a space he could see the blond woman at the wheel. His limbs were so heavy, all he could do was watch. Then the shivering started. This must be shock. Or whatever comes after shock. If his bowels let go, he would know he was dead and this was hell.

The motion of the boat became more violent. They must have cleared the point. The woman turned the boat and lashed the wheel in place. Then she pushed the throttle to full. As the engine roared and the hull battered its way uncertainly through the waves, the woman staggered to the rail and dove over.

As the boat cleared the top of a large wave, everything on the deck seemed to float, as if gravity had been repealed. Then gravity came back with a vengeance. Reeling from the impact, Hobbs sputtered as water poured over the bow and sides. Alan's body rolled away from him.

Hobbs tried to stand, but it was no good. The corkscrewing of the boat in the waves, the wind, the torrent of rain all conspired to cause him to slam into the deck once again. Then, plunging through the waves, the deck slammed him back. He felt the blackness closing in again. He felt at peace, and suddenly the storm felt very far away. He couldn't imagine what it was that held him to the world, but he could feel it draw thin.

He watched the bodies and rushing water lift free from the deck again. He felt himself weightless for another instant and did not care. Then all of it came crashing down again. A side locker exploded with the impact and discharged fishing gear and equipment onto the deck. In the debris, Hobbs's hands found a life preserver. Then the deck crashed down again. Time skipped.

When Hobbs opened his eyes again, he had no idea how long he had been out. Probably a blink. Maybe an hour. But he still clutched the life preserver to his chest. With his left hand, he reached the side rail and pulled. He got his feet underneath him, but couldn't push hard enough to stand. He waited until the top of another wave, until everything went weightless again, then pushed himself over the side.

The water welcomed him with a wet, concrete slap. Then it melted and sucked him in. The sting of the salt on his wounds was enough to revive him. Force him to cry out, and suck air and water. He coughed and clawed the water around him. He had lost the life preserver. The impact had torn it from his hand, and he struggled to stay afloat. His thrashing grew weak and feeble.

A flash of lightning illuminated the sky and was all the more terrifying for the blackness of the ocean it revealed. His head went under, and the roaring of the ocean seemed to call his name.

The sea spit him up again, and he shook his head, coughing. The side of his face bumped into the life jacket. And he knocked it away as he clawed for it. He swam after it, but it drifted farther away. All strength left him. As another wave lifted him up, he resigned himself to death.

At the crest of the wave, the wind caught the corner of the life jacket and blew it back to him.

He put one arm in, and then the other. He struggled to buckle the straps. He whimpered in rage and impotence, for he could not scream. One of the straps clicked, and then he had no more to give. He drifted as the waves turned to mountains, the wind to water, and the full fury of the hurricane hammered into the Florida coast, taking him with it.

EIGHT

Then Hobbs was on the beach. The sun was shining and he knew he was alive because he was in a lot of pain. He turned his head and watched a car go by on the other side of some scrubby dunes.

Somehow he stood. His need for water overwhelmed his need for rest. He half crawled across the dunes and managed to stand in the middle of the road. Just another piece of flotsam scattered across the tarmac. He started walking. A National Guard truck, a big deuce and a half, pulled up alongside him. One of the guardsmen called down to him from the cab, "You a looter?"

"No," said Hobbs, because it was the truth. He'd tried. But he hadn't looted a damn thing.

They lifted him into the back of the truck and he passed out. When he woke again, he was in a makeshift hospital in Apalachicola. He checked his stomach. It had been stitched up, messily and quickly, but somebody had operated on him. Then he passed out again. Three days later, when he could stand, he stole some clothes and slipped out of the hospital with a bottle of pain pills. An awful lot of money had gone missing, and, hurricane or no, people would start asking some pretty serious questions about a John Doe with a gunshot wound.

He stole a car from an empty house and headed north in a haze. He never would remember the path he'd taken through the twisty back roads and forgotten towns of middle Georgia. He'd just headed north until he hit US 1. Somewhere in there he had robbed a convenience store in a cinder-block building with a Laundromat. It was the middle of the night, and when he leaned on the counter, an evil-faced, chain-smoking woman asked him if he was all right. He leaned in as if he were going to tell her a secret, the reek of fifty years of Pall Malls filling his nose. The he hit her behind the ear with a left hook she never saw coming. She went down, pulling an overfull ashtray on top of her as she went.

He didn't feel good about it, but he felt worse about the fact that the register only had sixty-seven dollars in it. He thought about getting something to eat, but the smell of cigarettes and the red, dying glow of the jar of pickled eggs next to the cash register caused his gut to do flips. He turned on the pumps and crunched the last of the pills as he pumped the gas.

He must have had some kind of a plan, but on the other side of all that fear and rage and stale, shaky adrenaline, he couldn't have told you what it was.

He coasted into Charlotte on fumes. Feeling like an old tree that had rotted away from the inside. He eased off I-77 and headed away from the bright lights of the downtown. He pulled into the parking lot of a place with a sign that said, "Chicken and Ribs." Food, just needed some food.

At first he had thought the gnawing pain in his gut had caused him to sweat through his clothes, but then he realized that he had bled through his bandage and the stolen shirt. Couldn't go into a restaurant like that. Probably couldn't hit a drive-through. He tried to think of a way around this, but even as the gears in his brain tried to mesh, his body stepped in and said, enough.

His eyes closed for him.

That was the last thing he remembered until he woke up in the rest home. Wasn't hard to fill in the blanks, though. Somebody had rolled him for thirty-four dollars and a stolen car with Florida plates. Well, fuck them too.

PART FOUR
GIRL VERSUS BOYS

ONE

Special Agent Barry Leproate worked in the Purgatory field office of the FBI. It was hot in Jacksonville, Florida, but not hot enough to kill you. It was nicer than, say, Buffalo, he supposed, but probably less exciting. Mostly Purgatory involved paperwork. Never ending, always the same. Sometimes there were people to be interviewed, but mostly it was financial records that needed scouring.

A year and a half ago he had gotten to slap cuffs on a suspect while he was trying to shred evidence. He had joked with his boss that he should have gotten hazard pay due to the risk of paper cuts. His boss had almost laughed. The FBI was not known for a sense of humor, but when the work was this dry and boring, you did what you could to get through.

It was all pointless in the way that only the machinations of large bureaucracies can be pointless. Leproate knew there were criminals out there. People stealing and swindling from the American taxpayer on a scale that boggled the imagination. There still had been no prosecutions from the 2008 financial crisis. Leproate didn't know which bankers were guilty, but he knew some of them were. Maybe all of them were. Maybe it was just too big, too horrifying to uncover? Steal a dollar and it's a crime. Steal a few trillion and it's a statistic?

Leproate tried not to think about things like that. But in Purgatory he had a lot of time on his hands.

It hadn't always been this way. Leproate had once been a rising star, hot shit with a federal badge. But he'd screwed up. And they'd sent him to Purgatory. He tried not to think about that either. In fact, he tried not to think of anything but the top piece of paper on his desk and going home and enjoying the weekend with his wife and two kids.

It was, Leproate imagined, like doing time. You kept your head down and one day they would let you go back to the world. Getting excited about that would just make doing time more agonizing. Don't hope. Don't dream. Just do the time.

Most of the time, this strategy worked for him. But his old partner, Dan Tunks, had just gotten reassigned to San Francisco. A beautiful city, a paradise of a place, and all manner of real and interesting cases to work on. Not interstate wire fraud. So every time he looked up, Tunks's empty desk served as a reminder that escape was possible, but denied to him. And worse, the pile of paperwork on *his* desk had grown as a result. Same workload, but only one agent until the FBI saw fit to send him a new partner. How long would it be before someone screwed up badly enough to get stuck with this job? It took about two weeks.

His new partner was a woman. Blond, and would have been attractive, except for the rage in her eyes. Tight, angry eyes you wouldn't be surprised to see behind the bars of a cage. Her name was Wellsley, and even though he didn't know the particulars, he knew she had screwed up somehow. Maybe worse than he had, if such a thing was possible. She didn't seem to know she had screwed up. In fact, he could see she thought she had done the *right* thing. He read her as hell-bent on self-destruction.

Worst of all, she was young. Had she really been out of the academy long enough to screw up that badly? Evidently. Maybe she'd fuck up again and make him look good by comparison. Maybe she'd fuck up again and drag him down with her.

Leproate decided to let her have all the rope he could. He played it cool in the initial meeting. He was a quiet man anyway. He shook her hand. He said it was nice to be working with her, even though he could feel the floor sinking under his feet. The ASAC did most of the talking. He finished up with as much of a pep talk as he could muster: "I'm not going to tell you it's exciting work, Agent Wellsley—but it's important, and it needs to be done right."

When they got back to their desks, Leproate said, "Here we are. Give me a couple of minutes to straighten this out and I'll take you to lunch."

Wellsley stood there, bathed in the pale fluorescent light, staring at the gray-green industrial desk, and becoming well and truly whelmed by the magnitude of paperwork on it.

"Welcome to hell," she muttered.

"Oh no," said Barry Leproate, closing a folder, "this is Purgatory."

When Wellsley didn't smile, the bottom fell out of Agent Leproate's sinking feeling.

TWO

A Catholic school upbringing had taught Leproate that nobody stayed in Purgatory forever. So he bided his time and maintained his condition. Every working morning, he got up early (before the heat, but never early enough to beat the humidity) and ran sprints. In his neighborhood of identical houses on identical streets all named for trees that would not grow naturally in Florida, he would sprint one block on, one block off. He would run as fast as he could, putting all the passion and the rage into one explosion of motion, then jog a block and hope he wasn't having a heart attack.

He never stopped. He rarely walked. Stopping just made it harder not to throw up in the intervals. Not that Leproate would have minded. That was part of the game, but he didn't want the embarrassment of throwing up in front of a neighbor's house. Still, sometimes it happened.

Sometimes—when the early morning was still, and the air was cool, and it seemed as if all of life had been put on pause—he thought that he might be able to outrun the past. The shame and stupidity of what he had done. But it never worked. No matter how far or how fast he ran, his memory never changed.

When he got back to the house, Jennifer was cleaning up from breakfast and the daily tornado of getting the boys out the door to the bus stop.

Jennifer said to him, "When are you going to bring your new partner home for dinner? I want to meet him."

"Her," said Leproate, trying to not to wince in anticipation.

"Her? You didn't say anything about a *her* last night!"

"I did," he lied, "you just didn't hear me." *Jesus Christ. Nobody on Earth can outrun this.*

"Well, now you have to bring her."

"OK," said Leproate, putting the empty glass in the sink, "but you won't like her."

"Don't you like her too much either," snapped Jennifer.

"Honey, hand to God, I hate her already."

Jennifer held his gaze, then turned back to the garbage can. As she pulled the drawstrings on the trash bag tight, she muttered, "I don't know why any woman would *want* to join the FBI."

Neither did Leproate. Neither did most of the guys they worked with, but, political correctness being what it was, everybody tended to keep his mouth shut about it until after the third beer.

When the dinner finally happened, it was horrible. Wellsley dressed like a soldier who had been deployed for so long she had forgotten what civilians wore. No makeup. Jeans and a polo shirt. Not a girly thing about any of it, but somehow that only served to make it worse. Trying not to call attention to how beautiful she was just amplified the youthful, animal beauty of her athletic body.

She moved with all of the grace and rhythm that Jennifer lacked—had never had, in fact. Jennifer took it, and everything else, personally. Especially the fact that the boys were fascinated by Agent Wellsley.

"Have you ever shot anybody?" Rob asked.

"Have you ever *killed* anybody?" demanded John-Matthew, always trying to outdo his older brother.

Wellsley paused as if she was afraid of the attention, and looked to Leproate for an answer. He just smiled and shrugged. *Do what you want.* He was amused to see his angry new partner show her humanity for a change.

As Wellsley opened her mouth to speak, Jennifer snapped, "Young men, we don't talk about things like that with our guests. Now go wash your hands."

As the boys scampered off, Wellsley, said, "Oh, it's OK—" but she was cut off.

"Well," asked Jennifer, "have you?"

This time Wellsley did not look to Leproate for guidance. "Yes," she answered. "Does that make you feel better, or worse?"

"Better. I wouldn't want my husband to have a weak partner."

Wellsley said, "I'm not weak," in the same way that she might have stated any other obvious fact. Like, "It's raining" or "That door opens outward."

Jennifer looked away first. She muttered, "Better than the last one," as she padded back into the kitchen, but she didn't sound as if she had convinced herself.

Afterward they finished the uninspired meal of pork chops and pasta. Well, everyone except Wellsley had pasta. When Jennifer had set the bowl down, she had said, "Nothing fancy," in a way that fished for a compliment.

Wellsley said, "I'm sorry, I don't eat pasta."

There was an awkward good-bye at the door. Wellsley tried, "You have a lovely family," but it was such a strain, Leproate thought he heard one of her molars crack with the effort.

When the round, sedentary softness of his wife slid into bed next to him, she said, "That woman has to be a lesbian. She didn't have a stitch of makeup on."

"Whatever she is," said Leproate, "I can tell you one thing, she hates men."

"Lucky you," Jennifer said. And soon after, her breathing changed and Leproate knew she was asleep. He lay awake for a long time, thinking of what Jill Wellsley looked like naked, and hating himself for it.

THREE

The next day Leproate skipped his run and got to the office early. Wellsley had a deposition that took all morning. When she finally got done, it was after lunch. Leproate said, "I'm sorry about last night."

"What? Why?" asked Wellsley, all business.

"I hate those fucking pork chops."

For the briefest of instants, Wellsley smiled. But it was interrupted by ASAC Harberg. He didn't say a word. He just pointed at the conference room. They followed.

The first thing out of his mouth was, "Pack your shit, you'll run it out of Tallahassee."

Wellsley asked, "Run what?" but Leproate already knew. *Hot damn.*

"Somebody flipped an armadillo," said Harberg.

"What?" asked Wellsley, totally perplexed.

"We think somebody hit an armored car. Twenty-three million dollars," said Harberg.

Leproate whistled low. "We have the truck?"

"No, it's gone. Moonis-Brainerd lost contact with it about an hour and a half ago. It's twenty minutes late to its first stop in Apalachicola." He slid the folder across the table toward Leproate. "You'll run it. You want back in the bureau's good graces, this is your shot."

"Why is he in charge?" Wellsley asked.

"Because I said so," said Harberg.

"Is this discrimination?" Wellsley asked, not veiling her threat very much. Leproate rubbed his eyes.

Harberg considered Wellsley for a moment. "The word's out about you, Agent. I don't know if the word is right, but I'm gonna tell you two things anyway. One, if you decide this job isn't for you, you can quit anytime you want, and it might be better for everybody if you did. Do you want to work for the FBI?"

Wellsley, sounding small, said, "Yes, sir."

"Two, this broken-down old wreck of a partner of yours may quite possibly know more about armos than anybody else we've got. There was a time, before he shot himself in the foot, when he was the go-to man. So if you shut up and follow his lead, you just *might* learn something."

Wellsley shut up. Nobody was convinced that she was going to follow Leproate's lead.

As they packed up, Harberg pulled him aside. "Look, if she goes all Billie Jean King on you, you let me know and I'll pull her."

Leproate said, "Boss, Billie Jean King could *play.*"

"You know what I mean. If she ain't FBI, she ain't. Nothing you can do about it."

"I know, but let's give her some rope and see where she goes."

"Just make sure she doesn't hang you with it," said Harberg.

On the ride to Tallahassee, Leproate felt the anger radiating from Wellsley. He avoided the matter by spending most of his time on the phone. For a second he thought about telling her that she was hot when she was angry. Not because it was true, though it was, but because it might be fun to see her blow her stack. But then again, the car might not survive the explosion.

When they got to the Florida Highway Patrol HQ in Tallahassee, it already had a war room set up. And ten minutes after they walked into it, it was standing room only and Leproate was giving the rundown.

"I am Special Agent Leproate, this is Special Agent Wellsley. We will be coordinating this investigation and are grateful for all the assistance you have just been ordered to provide." This got a chuckle out of the room. Leproate had seen other agents come down all Charlie Hard-Ass in situations like this, but he believed that people would try harder for you if you weren't an asshole to them.

"We have a missing, presumed stolen, Moonis-Brainerd armored car. Last we knew of it, it passed through Medart headed south on 319. It never made its first scheduled stop in Apalachicola. Giving us a search area from Panama City east to Branford and north to Thomasville, Georgia. Somebody keep an eye out the window, they might drive by.

"We've got three coast guard cutters on patrol in the Gulf and an E-2C plane on loan from Miami. Nothing gets on the Gulf without being searched.

"FBI evidence techs are working on stoplight cameras and surveillance footage and tracker data from the truck itself. But y'all know better than me, once you get south of here, it gets pretty wild.

"I've got a list of people we want help questioning. And I want a sweep of the area. It's late for roadblocks, so we've got BOLOs clear across to Texas and all the way up to Atlanta just in case. There's twenty-three million dollars out there somewhere. And the people who stole it. Let's go find them."

The meeting broke up. Leproate glad-handed the troopers for a little while. Some he knew, some he was glad to meet. One or two of them walked over to the far corner of the room and made an effort to introduce themselves to Wellsley. Leproate thought nothing of it. He was exchanging a word with Jim Cummings, a giant of a man who had helped him out a few years back.

Wellsley's voice rose in anger. "That is *not* appropriate!" A few strained chuckles followed. Jim turned and Leproate could see the rest of the room. Wellsley was alone in her corner with a look of righteous indignation.

"What was that?" Jim rumbled.

"She's a bit high-strung."

Jim chuckled. "Good luck."

Leproate crossed the room. Before he could even ask, Wellsley said, "Did you see the way they treated me?"

"I didn't notice anything special."

"Two of them hit on me! I'm a goddamned FBI agent."

"Y'know, some people would take that as a compliment."

"And others would call that harassment! We've got a job to do. Am I never going to be clear of this bullshit? Who do I have to castrate to get respect?"

Leproate took a deep breath. *Don't look at her breasts*, he thought to himself. *Do not look at her breasts under that tight button-down shirt.* Why did women do these things to men? Leproate said, "I'm not sure that would…"

"And they all called me ma'am!"

"Ma'am, in this part of the country, that's called being polite."

"In any part of the country, that's called being unprofessional. I am not a *ma'am*. I am a *special agent* of the *Federal Bureau of Investigation*. They should call me Agent, not ma'am."

Leproate sighed. "It doesn't always have to be a fight."

"That's easy for you to say. You don't have to deal with all the bullshit I have to. And forget about it if I was African American."

"What is your intention here, Agent Ma'am?"

She hit him in the mouth.

Leproate rode the punch by taking a step back. He lifted a hand to his lip, and when he took it away, it was bloody. Wellsley glared a challenge. He heard a snicker from the knot of guys over by the door. He ignored them, but was grateful to hear the door shutting behind them as they left.

Leproate asked, "You feel better now that you got that out of your system? Or you need to castrate me?"

She didn't answer. She breathed heavily, hands tight, ready for a fight.

"Agent Wellsley, believe it or not, I have never hit a woman. But if you do that again, I am going to make one hell of an exception to that rule."

"You know how condescending that is? You think I can't fight? Poor little defenseless woman!"

Holy shit she was angry! A deep anger that smoldered in her bones. Barry's eyes flicked to the Glock on her hip, then back to her lovely face, contorted in rage. He lowered his voice.

"I know you can fight. I'm *sayin'* I don't *want* to fight you." He could see that it didn't even make a dent. "OK, Agent Ma'am. You want to beat the hell out of me, go ahead."

"What?"

"Go ahead, get it out of your system. I've had my ass kicked before. I lived." At this Wellsley calmed down, just a little bit. A little bit was better than nothing. "Agent, my intention is to catch whoever stole all that money. Because that's the job. What is your intention?"

"It's not right," she said through clenched teeth.

"The job, or the rest of it?"

"The rest of it, all this patriarchal bullshit. It's wrong. It's fucking wrong and it's tearing the world apart."

"Well, what do you want me to do about it?" Leproate kept speaking so she wouldn't have a chance to answer. That was one question he wanted to stay well and truly rhetorical. "There's a lot wrong with the world and most of it I can't do a damn thing about. But I can do something about this robbery. That is something I can fix. But I can't do it without your help. And I can't do it if you piss off the entire State of Florida."

"If I'm going to work, I need to be treated with respect."

"No argument. But they were respecting you, just not the way you see fit. I mean, goddamn, it's not like anybody patted you on the ass."

And right there Leproate thought she might shoot him. Wellsley held it together, saying through her teeth, "There's all kinds of sexism."

"And I can't do a thing about any of it. Now, you want to get down to work?"

FOUR

Wellsley didn't want to get down to work. Instead she left. Twenty minutes later she called and attempted to apologize. Well, maybe that's what Leproate could have called it. She was now headed to the local Moonis-Brainerd armored car depot to interview (and hopefully not piss off) everybody there. It needed to be done. But Leproate didn't hold high hopes for any breakthroughs.

Leproate put his head down and worked the case. He was going to get what he needed, one way or another. Late that afternoon, ASAC Harberg called him on his cell. Leproate gave him the update. Then Harberg asked, "How is it with Billie Jean King?"

Leproate answered without thinking about it, "Good. Little rough around the edges, but she's working her end."

"Yeah," said Harberg. "You watch her."

Leproate killed the call and walked down the hallway to where three techs were scouring video surveillance.

Leproate said, "Whattya got?"

The middle tech hit pause and looked up at Leproate. "All I can see so far is they loaded up the truck and left."

"Smart money is on an inside job," said Leproate.

"I ain't arguing that, Agent, I'm just sayin' from what we can see in the evidence, smart money might be betting against the house."

Leproate nodded.

"We've got clips of the truck leaving Tallahassee. I scoured a clip from a Walmart security camera in Crawfordville. So far that's it."

"OK," said Leproate, "Uncle Sam has got full overtime for two days. I'm signing all the checks, so if you don't stay up all night, I'll find somebody who will."

"Where's that pretty partner of yours?"

Leproate said, "We're working shifts."

"Is she taking the night shift?" said the tech with a stupid, suggestive leer.

"She's a federal agent. I'm pretty sure she'll shoot you if you say that to her. And I'm pretty sure she'll get away with it."

He went back into the war room and sat looking at his laptop. His stomach had turned sour from all the coffee. When he burped up a little acid, he opened his bag and pulled out a bottle of Pepto-Bismol. Leproate took a slug right from the bottle and then started tapping questions into the National Crime Information Center database. It was hard because he wasn't too good with computers, but eventually he got a list of reports to page through.

As he read them, his eyes grew bleary and his stomach pained him again. He should really sleep, but this was a *case*. He wanted to close this one so badly he would have been able to taste it, if not for the stomach acid. He hit the bottle again and left the top off when he set it down. He was gonna need it again for sure. And more coffee, God help him. For a moment he wondered if he could use Pepto as creamer and get both drug effects at once. Then he saw it.

He got up so fast, he knocked over the bottle of Pepto-Bismol and left it running out over the conference room table.

He collected Wellsley at the hotel. She was the kind that wakes up slowly. Leproate waited until she was in the car to explain.

"It's not an inside job."

"I didn't find anything to suggest that. One of the guys was cheating on his wife, but nobody was preparing to leave."

"On that Loomis Fargo heist in North Carolina, the agents knew it was an inside job the first time they watched the tapes. They literally saw one guy loading his personal truck with cash and driving off. The rest was just finding him."

"They were amateurs, idiots, right?" asked Wellsley.

"Yeah, the guy who actually stole the money was rooked out of his share. The people who got it spent it like idiots. Bought a big house. ATVs. They even filled a wine cellar with box wine. You know what white trash is, Agent Wellsley?" Leproate asked, letting his Southern accent manufacture extra syllables in her name.

"I've heard of it."

"That right there is the very definition of white trash. Box wine in the cellar of a million-dollar house."

"Why did you get me out of bed?"

"Well, Agent, before my fall from grace, I was a man much in demand in the bureau because of my expertise with armored car robberies."

"Flipped armadillos?"

"Yeah, well, that's just one kind. A failed kind. See, back in the thirties, this gang hit a truck out in Nevada. They got the driver, but the two men in the back wouldn't open up. Men"—he looked over at Wellsley and added, "and women, being made of sterner stuff in those days.

"Now the robbers didn't have anything to open the rear compartment, but they weren't in any particular kind of a hurry. So they drove the truck way out into the desert—the Mojave Desert—and attempted to reason with the men in the back of the truck. At first it was a fruitless negotiation. But as the sun came up and beat down on the truck, the robbers thought that the men inside would soon change their tune. Literally sweat them out.

"But somewhere in there, somebody misestimated. See, the Mojave gets hot. Holds the record for highest land temperature ever recorded in North America, 134 degrees. Now I don't know how hot it was that day, but before the men inside the truck had time to come to their senses, they were overcome by heatstroke and died."

"What's this have to do with this case?"

"Well, the robbers didn't give up. They took the truck to the nearest cliff they could find and rolled it off the edge, thinking, presumably, that the cargo portion would burst open and they would make a getaway."

"But the truck wouldn't open."

"No, and that's where it was found, six days later, and where legendary US marshal John Leonard declared, 'Them boys were roasted, just like a flipped armadillo.'"

"Colorful, but what's the point?"

Leproate sighed. That's what was wrong with Yankees, no appreciation of history. "There's all kinds of ways to steal an armored car. And they've changed over the years. But about the time of my...mistake, the armored car companies won. Between GPS and video cameras and dye packs and recording the serial numbers—it just became more trouble than it was worth to take an armored car. So the pros stopped trying.

"So you're saying professionals didn't take our truck?"

"There was this man, best thief I ever heard of. He was called Hobbs, but there's no way that's his real name. About twenty-five years ago he went on a streak. Fifteen armored cars in a row. I'm pretty sure I've been chasing him and his copycats most of my career. I think this one ol' boy, all on his own, came up with three or four new ways to crack an armadillo. One of which was stealing one and putting propane torches underneath it to heat it up and get the guys inside to open up. Hot enough to sweat them, but not hot enough to kill them."

"GPS defeats that?"

"Yes, ma'am. Yes, *Agent*. With GPS there's not enough time to get it all set up and sweat them out. We caught two crews before word got out, but we didn't get Hobbs. But here's the thing. Each time the ol' boy changed his technique, he did a practice run. Or part of one. Because if you were going to try something totally new, what would you do?"

"I'd test it to see if it works first."

"So I looked up every crime report that mentions an armored car in the United States in the last year. And what pops up, but the theft of an *empty* armored car from a refitting company in Saint Louis two months ago."

"So to find a stolen armored car full of money, we're going to start with a stolen armored car that's empty?"

"Yes, we are."

They flashed badges through security and boarded a regional jet as the sun came up. Wellsley leaned against the window and was asleep almost instantly. Leproate envied that. Maybe it was youth. Now that she was unguarded, he watched her as she slept.

She was a creature, wild and fierce. Nothing like his well-padded and domesticated wife. Before he fell asleep, Leproate's second-to-last thought was, *I should call Jennifer when we land.* His last thought was about having sex with his new partner.

FIVE

The man who owned Regent Armored, Daniel McCaffery, made a point of saying, “I’m the official king of Regent Armored,” as often as he could. Leproate doubted that the line would ever be funny, but now, given the heavy bruises down the side of McCaffery’s face, it was just sad. He looked like the official king of taking a beating.

Leproate ran through all the usual angles—disgruntled employees, competitors, known enemies. Nothing fit. The guy who’d swiped the truck had been young, but all of this felt to Leproate like the work of someone who knew what he was doing.

Leproate and Wellsley split up everyone who had worked the shift that night, and interviewed them separately. When they were done, he didn’t have to ask her. She shrugged and he knew. They had nothing. Not even the guy who’d gotten sapped on the sidewalk could give them a description.

They bagged the surveillance camera’s hard drive and stepped outside into the late afternoon.

“So,” said Wellsley, “you might be right, but I don’t see how it gets us anywhere.”

Leproate scanned the street, head on a swivel. “Why didn’t they catch the kid in the armored car?”

Wellsley nodded, getting it. “Yeah. They call the cops, everybody is looking for it…a slow, obvious vehicle. How did he get away?”

Leproate looked at the decaying industrial district that surrounded them. Across the street was a five-story brick building that took up the whole block. The double doors were closed with a padlock and chain. All the windows were broken out. Even the panes on the top floor. Must have been done from the inside. It'd be real work to pull that off from street level. Vandals wouldn't have that kind of work ethic. They would have the time. Scumbags have nothing but time.

"They didn't get away," Leproate realized out loud.

"But they weren't caught?"

Agent Leproate was already walking away, right down the middle of the street. "They headed away from the river." He stood in the first intersection. To the right he could see the river cutting northeast across the grid of the city. North were more surface streets, abandoned warehouses, and factories. "Ennh...left turn." He continued walking.

"Is this some kind of Jedi mind trick?" asked Wellsley. "Because I don't remember them teaching this at Quantico."

The next intersection went all four ways. Barry sighed and stood there for a minute. Wellsley said, "If you are that serious about it, we should get some help and have all of these buildings searched. Get it done quickly."

Leproate asked himself, "Which building would I use? And why? Big enough...and I would have needed to scout the job." He turned left again and walked quickly. In the middle of the block, when he saw the alley leading into the center of the large brick complex across the street from Regent Armored, he knew.

"This one."

"Bullshit," said Wellsley. Then she followed him in.

Leproate's voice rang off the brick walls of the alleyway. "They would have scouted it from up there. And if there was a place, they would have stashed the truck here, even holed up for a while."

In the far wall of the courtyard was a large sliding metal door, the kind with counterweights. It had been battered to shit, but it opened easily and without a sound.

The light of the setting sun came through the alley behind Leproate and illuminated the large room on the other side of the door. There, cut through the dirt and refuse on the ancient factory floor, were skid marks from where a large, heavy truck had come to a short stop. Wadded up in the corner were several large tarps.

"How the fuck did you do that?" asked Wellsley.

"Call them," said Leproate. "Call everybody."

SIX

Late, late that night, Leproate lay on the bed in his motel room and stared at the ceiling. At first he didn't know why he couldn't fall asleep. Then he recognized the reason as excitement. It had been so long since he had been so excited about a case that he had forgotten the name of the feeling.

He still hadn't talked to his wife. She had called twice and left a message that he hadn't listened to. He felt strange about this, maybe even bad, but he hadn't done anything about it. Now it was too late.

There was a knock on the door.

He opened it. It was Wellsley. She stood there for a moment, wearing a T-shirt and her suit pants, saying nothing. Her eyes were red, maybe from crying, maybe from lack of sleep. Her hair tousled from turning and turning on a hotel-room pillow. She bit her upper lip and let it go. It should have been awkward, not sexy, but this show of vulnerability somehow made her human. The sight of her nipples poking through the T-shirt sent a shiver of guilty schoolboy pleasure racing through him. With an effort he pulled his gaze back up.

"I don't want to make a big deal out of this," she said, looking either way down the long hallway.

Leproate parted his lips to say, "OK," and she stepped into the room and kissed him. Hard. A grinding punch-in-the-lips of a kiss. She drove him backward and the door shut behind them.

"Hey, hey," he mumbled, but she pushed him onto the bed.

"I need this," she said. And then he felt her press a gun into the side of his head.

"What the fuck?"

She kissed him and the steel pressed harder. She broke the kiss with a giggle, a horrible, brittle sound that scared him. But not all of him. He was harder than he had been in years.

She leaned back and held the gun on him. She smiled, almost apologetically, and said, "Don't make a sound."

From her back pocket, she produced a knife. The spring-assisted blade snapped open and she slipped it under his waistband. He gasped at the touch of steel along the inside of his left leg. She sliced and then his sweatpants and boxers weren't in the way anymore.

She leaned back farther, grinding her pelvis hard into him, and repeated the same trick with her pants. He felt the tip of the knife graze his belly, and when he looked down a thin cut welled with a trace of blood.

She pressed her forehead to his chest and slid it forward, using her forehead to pin him by the throat on the bed. He heard fabric ripping and then she slid her hips down and took him inside her.

She rode him slowly at first, and then with a ferocity that scared him. It felt great. Was this crazy bitch gonna kill him? Oh God, it felt great. This crazy bitch was going to kill him.

She made tiny, mewling cries, weak and soft, in contrast to the sexual assault that was blowing his mind.

When he came he cried out and she cracked him across the face with the gun. She choked him with her left hand and rode him all the harder. Leproate bit the inside of his cheek to stay quiet and everything went white for a while.

She made a violent, spasming finish, and he felt the grip on his throat relax. He heard her panting and opened his eyes. All he saw was the cold, black hole of a .40-caliber muzzle pointed right at his face. It was a small thing, but pointed at him, it looked big enough to swallow his whole world.

From beyond the gun, she said, "Don't fucking move."

Yes, ma'am, he thought, realizing that he was out of breath.

She got up, wrapped a towel around her shredded pants, and left.

Leproate lay on the bed, panting, excited, satisfied, and very afraid. When he stopped shaking, he got up and looked at his face in the mirror.

"What the fuck was that?"

He was still asking himself as he fell asleep.

SEVEN

The next morning it might have all been a dream, except for the bruise on his temple and the raw patch on his throat. Wellsley had said, "Good morning," and nothing else. Every bit as cold and distant as she had ever been. In a way he was grateful he wasn't sitting next to her on the plane flight back. He was confused. He had no idea how to feel about any of this. Cheap airline coffee, guilt, and lust churned around in his stomach all the way back to Tallahassee.

He still hadn't called his wife. How could he? What would he say? She would hear in his voice that something was wrong. He didn't know what she would assume, but it would be bad. She would probably worry about him. She always worried about him when he was away. That he would be in danger, be shot on the job. A flash of pleasure through his loins and the image of Wellsley's athletic, gyrating body on the other side of the .40-caliber muzzle.

He shook his head and tried to get a handle on things.

By the time the plane landed, he had almost convinced himself he was in the catbird seat. He was running a shit-hot case, had a hot partner whom he was banging. Sure she was crazy, but that added to the spice. After years of boredom and drudgery, life was finally paying him back. He walked quickly through the airport, but couldn't outrace the doubts. *Focus on the case*, he thought. *Just focus on the case.*

When they got back to the war room at the Florida Highway Patrol HQ in Tallahassee, everything had fallen apart. The video techs were gone and the walls were bare. A trooper said, "Don't worry, we put everything in a box for you after we took it down."

"Why'd you take it down?"

"Game was called on account of rain," said the trooper.

"What the fuck are you talking about?" asked Leproate, his lack of sleep getting the best of him.

"Hurricane. Governor's declared a state of emergency."

"What?"

The trooper explained that in the last forty-eight hours a tropical storm had become a hurricane and was bearing down on the panhandle. How quickly your luck could change. Wellsley said, "I'll get the stuff," and left in search of the stuff.

Leproate and the trooper took a second to watch Wellsley walk away. Then got ASAC Harberg on the phone. "Boss, they shut us down," said Leproate.

"I know, Agent. Act of God, nothing the bureau can do."

"But boss, things are heating up. With what we got from Saint Louis, I think we can nail them if we get a little cooperation. They're sitting on it somewhere, waiting for things to cool off. If we can get one more piece of the puzzle."

"What you've got is a hunch. And I like your hunch. But there's nothing I can do. You are ordered to give the Florida Highway Patrol your full cooperation."

"There's twenty-three million dollars in the wind here. That's more than Dunbar. It's the largest armored car heist in US history. If we move now—"

"Agent, it's a shit-hot case, but a hurricane is gonna plow into the Gulf Coast. It'll tear hell clear up to Georgia. That could be billions in damages. Just pray to God New Orleans doesn't get pounded again."

"Game called on account of rain...," Leproate mumbled.

"What's that?"

"That's what a trooper just said to me."

"That's not exactly right. It's not a game, Agent, it's a series. We don't have to win them all, we just have to win most of them."

Leproate hung up the phone on the shittiest pep talk ever.

Wellsley came back into the room, carrying three boxes of their casework. She said, "The major asked us if we could stop by his office so he could have our cooperation."

Leproate said, "Follow me."

Out in the parking lot, she dropped the cases into the trunk. Leproate slid in behind the steering wheel.

"What about the major?"

"I don't have any cooperation to give right now. I'm going to drive around and try to find some," said Barry, surprised at how those words sounded in his voice. She slid into the passenger seat and smiled at him. For the first time since last night, she didn't look so sinister to him.

He wheeled out of the parking lot, following the flow of traffic, neither of them saying anything. Finally Wellsley said, "They're still there, right?"

"Probably."

"I mean, if that's their MO, then they're down there somewhere, waiting for the heat to pass."

"Yeah," said Leproate, "they don't know that the game was called on account of rain."

"Just because the FHP doesn't want to get muddy."

"What?"

"They've called a mandatory evacuation," said Wellsley.

Leproate nodded.

"Would you just leave twenty-three million dollars lying around?"

"No," said Leproate, "I'd wait until everybody else cleared out, and then split at the last minute, letting the storm cover my tracks. Everybody else running for cover, nobody standing out in the rain, looking in trunks."

"Or you might hunker down and wait out the whole thing. Either way…"

"There's always a few that stay behind," said Leproate.

"So we drive around, see who's left."

Leproate pulled into a supermarket parking lot. He opened the trunk and rummaged around until he found a map. He unfolded and refolded until it showed the panhandle. He drew a small circle around Sopchoppy. "Somewhere after this."

Wellsley leaned in close and he caught the smell of her. She was sexy without even meaning to be. Leproate enjoyed it anyway.

Wellsley took the pen and drew a wider circle. Panacea, Alligator Point, Carrabelle, Ochlockonee Pointe. It was a lot of territory. "It's big," he said.

She indicated Alligator Point. "Lotta rental houses around here. Wouldn't you want to stay on the beach?"

A fat raindrop hit the map with a surprising crack. Then another. Leproate folded the map up, and they got back into the car.

"Let's just go have a look. Maybe we get lucky," said Wellsley.

"Are you asking me?"

"You are the agent in charge," she said, her expression neutral.

He put the car in drive and turned south.

EIGHT

As they drove they heard that Hurricane Kristy had been upgraded to a category two. What had seemed like a good idea in Tallahassee felt worse as they drew toward the coast.

Leproate recognized the surreality of it. The steady flow of cars to the north as they flashed badges through checkpoint after checkpoint. One trooper told them, "I know you're FB of I, but I wouldn't stay down there long, unless you feel like getting washed out to sea."

Leproate thanked him and they drove on. In the mirror he could see the deputy shaking his head as they drove off. Maybe he was right.

Still, not everyone was fleeing. In the small town of Medart, they saw four young kids standing in front of a boarded-up convenience store. They cupped cheap, thin cigars against the wind. Just waiting for traffic to die down so they could loot the place, thought Leproate.

Wellsley rolled down her window and asked them, "You live here?"

"Can't afford to be from nowheres else," one of them said, and they all laughed. Their laughter sounded as if somebody had disturbed a murder of crows. Leproate drove on, taking a turn around the town. The only other people they saw were covering windows with boards and hunkering down for the storm. Shit poor, but citizens one and all. They drove on.

The farther south they went, the darker the sky became. Leproate said, "You know what it would mean if we nail these guys?"

"When," said Wellsley. "When we nail these guys."

But Leproate had doubts. They were off book here, for sure. And the FBI was a by-the-book organization. So far they could write this up and make it come out OK. Hell, everyone knew the rules could be bent, if you showed results. It was just like the army in that way. Sometimes it just wasn't possible to follow all the orders and get the job done.

But God help the soldier who broke the rules and didn't come through.

They drove south until they couldn't drive south anymore. Through the swamp, through scattered habitations and the occasional vacation home. On the long, open stretches of road the wind blew the car around more. Leproate began to feel more and more foolish.

They drove out onto the point, and the unbroken view of the approaching storm it granted them was a terrible thing to behold. Where the road bent, to the right, it looked as if the world had been swallowed up by a vengeful ocean and dragged into the maw of the storm. The waves crashed into the seawall and splashed onto the road. In the ocean beyond, flashes of lightning could be seen amid the darkness.

Wellsley touched him and said, "We've come this far." He knew it was foolish, but the gesture gave him strength.

As they drove along the beach a wave broke over the road. Just a fine spray on the windshield, but Leproate said, "We're gonna make this quick."

Wellsley said, "If they're here, they'll be easy to spot."

On the left, beach houses stood abandoned against the wrath of the storm. They were so close to the water, the storm was already sending waves into them. Nobody hiding in there. The isthmus widened, and Leproate took the next road to the right, heading toward the bay. They passed a number of fancy houses, built on stilts, with no sign of human life.

Leproate took another right and drove along a canal that led to the bay. Ahead was a cinder-block house nestled in the trees. The windows were boarded up, but the light in the carport spotlit a battered Subaru BRAT. A man stood next to it with a shotgun cradled under his arm and a bottle of beer in his hand.

They pulled up and he gave them a wave. And a skeptical look. They hurried under the shelter.

"What in the hell are you kids doin' out here? Don't you know there's a hurricane on?"

"FBI. Why haven't you evacuated?" Leproate demanded.

"Ain't got nowhere to go. Too old to care much. What's your excuse?"

"We're looking for men who robbed an armored car," Leproate said, feeling silly as he said it.

"Have you seen anything strange?" Wellsley asked.

The surf crashed against the beach on the seaward side of the point as the old man took a pull off the bottle of beer. He tossed the empty bottle into the back of the Subaru and squinted against the wind.

"Three guys I ain't seen leave yet, renting a house two turns down on the canal. Been here about a month. Never talk to nobody."

"Thank you," said Leproate.

As they got back into the car, the old man said, "You take care of that purty little lady."

NINE

"Condescending old fuck!" Wellsley said as she slammed the door.

"Forget about him," said Leproate as he started the car. He left the lights off and drove slowly, winding around the canal. When he got to the second turn, he saw the dock light flickering in the driving rain. He stopped the car.

"You ever done this before?" Leproate asked.

Jesus, he's losing his nerve, thought Wellsley. "Yeah, two-by-two cover."

"There's only two of us."

"Let's just go have a look. If there's only three of them."

"I just don't want...," Leproate said.

Oh, fucking spare me, Nancy boy, Wellsley thought. Rather than hear any more of this bullshit, she shoved out of the seat and took point.

They leapfrogged, using trees, the house next door, and finally a boathouse as cover. It didn't matter, thought Wellsley; who could see shit in this rain? All they could make out were shadows moving around a boat. What kind of person took a boat out in this weather? Nobody was that crazy. They had to be unloading the cash.

Leproate came up beside her on the boathouse wall. "How do you want to do this?" *Fucking finally*, she thought, *a man who will listen*. Although he had to fear for his life to come to his senses.

"You take the right, I'll take the left. We wait until they are all in the open, then order them to disarm."

"I've never...," he said, looking particularly lost with his thinning hair plastered to his forehead.

"Center mass, keep shooting until your target is down," said Wellsley, sounding irritated and not caring. "Look, you give the command, I'll shoot."

"Only if you have to...," said Leproate.

"Only if," she said, and peeled off to the left.

When she stepped out from behind the lee of the boathouse, she settled into the Weaver stance she'd been taught at Quantico. She held her gun lightly and easily, and let her feet glide across the ground as she watched the silhouettes of one of the men drift across her front sight.

Men. Her whole life it had been men. They held the power. They abused the power. And when you really needed them, they fell apart. Like what had happened with Dad after Mom died. And then there had been no one to protect her and Janet from the *men*.

A female high school teacher slept with one of her students and she went to jail. But a powerful man bought and sold little girls, and nothing happened to him. She was their victim and under their thumb everywhere she went. And why? They weren't stronger, they just had...money.

She heard Leproate yell, "Freeze, FBI!"

Four shapes in the darkness. Three bad men, and the fourth...her partner.

All three of the shapes in the darkness turned, and she could see their faces in the light above the dock. There were two old men and one young. Men. Men with money she could take. What would they do if she had the money and they wanted it? What had men always done to her?

She thought of Janet and pulled the trigger. Sometime after she dropped the first two, Leproate recovered from the shock enough to start shooting. When they were all down, she was aware of him yelling at her, but the waves beating against the shore were too loud for her to hear him. Then she realized it was her pulse. He was an idiot anyway. She needed to make sure they were all dead.

She hurried to the guy in the middle. He was still alive. The ugly black shape of a revolver lay on the sandy soil next to him. She picked it up.

Leproate was still making hysterically angry noises. She ignored his words. They didn't matter. She turned back and pointed at the ground next to the tall one. "Is that a weapon?"

When Leproate whirled, in fear for his life, she shot him in the back of the head. She resisted the urge to gloat, and hurried to the boat. She wanted to see it. The money. Her ticket out. Out from underneath the thumb of men forever.

The boat was empty.

She left the boat and went to check the vehicle, a large, crew-cab pickup truck with a cap on the back. As she passed the young man, she realized he was still alive, but in bad shape. She frisked him and took his gun as well. *Do everything in the right order*, she told herself. *First find the money.*

There was no money in the truck. They hadn't unloaded the armored car yet!

She went back to the young man. She asked him where the truck was. He said, "Fuck you." She shot him in the leg and stood on the wound for a while. His screams made her smile. Then she asked him again, already prepared to shoot him in the ankle next. Lots of nerve endings in the ankle.

This time he told her what she wanted to know. She thanked him. Then shot him in the face.

She left Barry where he was and loaded the bodies into the boat. Then she cast off and took the boat out into the canal. Where the bay opened up into the ocean, she pointed the craft directly into the storm. She lashed the wheel, opened the throttle, and dove into the water off the starboard side.

The Gulf was warm and, even with the waves, inviting. Wellsley was a strong swimmer, but she didn't need it. The waves carried her toward the shore. Mother Nature herself was helping her.

The waves tossed her up onto the beach, and she crawled and tumbled beyond the surf. She coughed for a while and cleared her throat of the salt water. Then she turned and looked at the line of storms bearing down on the coast. In the strange eddy that she found herself in before the edge of the hurricane, the sky was black, but there was no rain. The wind howled over the point and threatened to knock her from her feet.

She thought of all the people fleeing inland. All the people who hadn't fled, but huddled in the dark, afraid of this wall of chaos that roared down on her. The storm! The storm! She screamed into the wind. Crying out to the hurricane as sister. Breathless, she collapsed on the sand, thinking, *Now all those fleeing, huddling, faceless people know. Now they know how it feels to be me.*

She walked over a mile back to the house. The crime scene, she reminded herself. Leproate was where she'd left him. Good boy. She considered the scene for a while and decided it would play as it was. There was just one more loose end to tie up before she called in "Agent down."

This time the old man had the shotgun at high port as she drove up. Wellsley left the car running. She opened the door and stood. "Do you have a phone?"

"Jesus Christ, little lady, what happened? Sounded like a hell of a lot of shooting."

"I said, do you have a working phone?" Jesus, did men never listen?

"Yeah, sure," the old man said.

As Wellsley walked toward him, he repeated his question: "Was that gunfire?"

"Yes," she answered, and shot him three times in the chest. She walked over to where he lay on the ground, clutching his chest and leaking life into the sandy soil, and asked, "Is that purty enough for you, sweetheart?"

PART FIVE
AN END TO IT

ONE

Three months after

Wellsley and Detective Mazerick went into the garage, guns drawn. When she saw the hole knocked in the inside wall next to the garage door, her pulse jumped, and she had to remember to breathe. Mazerick crossed the cool darkness of the concrete floor and peeked through the hole. Then he waved her up with a nod of his head.

He stacked on the wall on the outside of the hole. She opened the door and saw his eyes go wide as she pushed through first. Didn't he think she could do this? She was goddamned FBI.

She saw the alarm keypad on the floor, surrounded by a scattering of plaster. He was here. He'd have to still be here, wouldn't he? An old man. Wounded, tired. They'd find him asleep someplace, for sure.

Except for the hole in the wall and the alarm system, the rest of the house was untouched. Like a house in a magazine. None of that shit that everybody had but nobody wanted to see. It was like a full-size dollhouse.

They cleared it quickly and quietly, finding only one staircase leading up. She had to give Mazerick this, he moved as if he knew what he was doing. At the first few corners, he looked back to check her, and smiled that asymmetric smile when he saw that she had her gun pointed in the right direction. As if he was proud of her, or just glad she wasn't going to accidentally shoot him. She could still taste that kiss and had to fight off the urge to spit.

They padded upstairs. The hallway at the top of the stairs went left and right. They looked at each other to decide a direction. Then they heard a noise from the left. It sounded like a muffled groan or a yawn.

Through that door was the master bedroom, and the bed had been slept in. It took an effort to check the corners and not stare at the bed. The unexpected is the hardest thing when you're clearing a room. Your brain wants to continue to look at the first new or unexpected thing you see, but it's the thing you don't see that will kill you.

She cleared the far side of the bed and nodded to Mazerick. He moved to the bathroom door. It was closed. He made a motion—*Should we kick it open?* Jackass. What was this, a TV show? She shook her head and pushed it lightly with the fingertips of her left hand. It swung noiselessly open onto a travertine floor.

The bathroom was like a cathedral, if cathedrals came with skylights, sunken tubs, and his and hers vanities. They heard the noise again, and it echoed in the empty bathroom. On the far side of the room was an open door.

Mazerick went first. As soon as he looked through the door, he started laughing. What the fuck? Wellsley checked the hallway behind her. That's where she would be if she were setting a trap. He kept laughing and she walked over and looked into the closet, gun still pointing toward the hallway.

On the floor were two men and a woman, tied with lamp cord and gagged with fabric.

"I think we missed him," Mazerick said. Then he laughed at his own obvious joke as if it were funny.

Wellsley knelt down beside the closest man and removed the gag. "Thank God you are here," he said. "I was showing the house, and there was a man. He attacked us. He stole my car."

"What kind of car?" asked Mazerick.

"An Escalade, but the stupid son of a bitch. He can't get away, you can track it with my phone."

Wellsley said, "Show me," and untied his hands.

The man dug around in his pockets and came up with a fancy phone. While he did, the couple beside him made whining noises through their gags. "Shhh," said Wellsley. "Do you want me to catch this guy or not?"

Mazerick was still chuckling as he undid the other man's gag. The first thing the guy said was, "Is my car all right, my Maserati? I was parked close behind."

Rich people, thought Wellsley. She'd have to remember to hate herself as soon as she became one.

The Realtor handed her his phone and she saw a map interface showing the location of his SUV. Heading south.

Mazerick reached for his radio, saying, "We got him!"

"Bang," said Wellsley's gun.

TWO

The Realtor stared at the spray of Mazerick's brains on the closet wall and ceiling. Then he screamed. His client repeated, "Ohmygodohmygodohmygodohmygod" over and over again. Wellsley was thankful that the woman was still gagged.

She hit the Realtor in the face and he stopped screaming. "What's the unlock code for the phone?"

"I-I-I-I," he stammered.

Wellsley interrupted him by firing her pistol again, the round passing right between his legs.

"Sixty-nine sixty-nine!" he screamed, and then turned his face away.

Wellsley locked the phone, then entered the code to verify that it worked. Then she shot all of them in the head. She felt bad about shooting the woman, but not very. She took the client's keys and stepped back into the bathroom.

She carefully ripped out a few of her hairs and sprinkled them onto the tile. She clawed at the closet doorframe until two of her nails broke. Then she lay down and kicked a hole in the drywall. She scattered some more of her hair by the bathroom door and went downstairs. Not much of an abduction scene, but she didn't think she'd need the time.

In the driveway was a Maserati Ghibli. Not a scratch on it. It looked as if it wouldn't have any trouble catching an SUV. She unlocked the phone and set it on the dash. She had to get him before he changed cars. The engine was smooth and powerful, a beautiful thing to hear. Before she put the car in gear, she remembered. Her cell phone went under the front of the rear wheel. Then she drove over it and away.

Wellsley took it slow out of the neighborhood, careful to avoid the patrol cops. Then she put her foot down and smiled at the roar. She knew she couldn't hold on to this car for long, but she would enjoy it while she could.

THREE

As she drove, her mind worked the angles. Her first thought was to catch him, get him to talk, plant the murder weapon on him, then bring him in. She could be the hero and still get the money. But that was what had gone wrong the last time. She had let herself be fooled by a lying man. That was *never* going to happen again.

Back on Alligator Point, her call of "Agent down" should have unleashed the full power and righteous fury of the FBI, but it hadn't. When she had finished explaining how all of it had been Agent Leproate's orders, she had been told to shelter in place. Nobody was sending anybody into the path of what was now a category three hurricane.

So she holed up, in that innocent old man's block house. The building had been there fifty years at least. No reason it wouldn't be there for fifty more. When the eye of the storm passed overhead, she came out for a look around. Most of the trees were gone. The old man's body had blown or been washed away someplace. The wind picked up again, and she didn't waste time looking for it. The house flooded, but the walls and roof stayed on.

They sent a Sea King search and rescue helicopter to pick her up with a medic and a field team. She told her story and it held, but they interrogated her as if they thought she was lying. In the end they put her on administrative leave pending further investigation. It was her word against nobody else's. They might not trust her, but what could they prove? One way or the other, it was effectively the end of her career with the FBI, but what did she care? She wasn't going to need a paycheck anymore.

She went to the location that she had gotten out of the kid. There she found a scummy pool of brackish water in the middle of the swamp. She stripped to her underwear and dove beneath the water. There, twenty feet below the surface, was the armored car.

She surfaced and hyperventilated, trying not to think about the alligators that most certainly lurked around this pool. When her bloodstream was full of oxygen, she dove all the way down.

The rear doors were open and the truck was empty.

She surfaced again, cursing. It was the truck from Saint Louis. She had killed five men and her career for nothing.

FOUR

When word got around that Wellsley was working the case on her own, from the outside, ASAC Harberg had warned her off. She told him to fuck off. That she was trying to avenge her dead partner. She made a big show of it, charging right into the field office. After that, one of the investigating agents, John Tabitha, had come to talk to her off the record.

From Agent Tabitha she learned that they still hadn't found the boat. She asked him for a copy of the case files. He agreed, but he said, "Two conditions. Don't ever tell them you got it from me. And if you get anything, it comes back to me."

He said the last part as an afterthought. As if the idea that she, a mere girl, could find something he had overlooked was beyond the realm of possibility. She hid her hatred and nodded as submissively as she could. Jesus, she was sick of playing the game.

She got another guy to run NCIS for all GSWs and all John Does admitted to hospitals after the hurricane. The emergency clinics were full of John Does. But almost all of these were quickly claimed and identified. Of the three remaining GSWs, two were looters. The last one had walked out of an emergency clinic in Apalachicola.

The trail was cold. Somewhere out there were millions of dollars that might never be found. Weeks passed. She told her story three more times to internal affairs, but there was no resolution in sight. So she lived in limbo. Running, reading the case file, looking at maps, going running again. She didn't sleep much.

That truck was down there somewhere. Lost amid the same unforgiving swamp where Ponce de León had looked for the Fountain of Youth. For his troubles, Ponce de León had died from a poisoned arrow in the leg. Doing a grid search would be like looking for a needle in an alligator-infested haystack. But still she lay awake at night and thought about trying.

Then she got a strange call. Her computer guy told her that, out of boredom, he had widened his search from 150 miles to four hundred. He got a hit in Charlotte, North Carolina. Tabitha had laughed at it. A guy found behind a Dumpster with multiple GSWs, days old. The hospital couldn't revive him. So they finally sent him to a state-run rest home. The tech had joked, "Well, he ain't going nowhere. He'll be there if you need him."

"Sure," said Wellsley, "I'll check it out." But by the time she got there, it was a murder scene. And Hobbs was gone.

But this time there would be no escape. She caught up with the Escalade just south of town. She got close enough to verify the pale, haggard man at the wheel, then she hung back about half a mile. She barely kept him in sight and relied on the tracker to do the rest.

She hung with him through Columbia, where he veered off onto US 1. Just shy of Augusta, he stopped for gas. She wondered if the old man was going to have to sleep anytime soon. She thought he might, but didn't count on anything. This was a long race and she would run it until the end.

Somewhere in the middle of Georgia, even the tracker wouldn't help her. It was late, and between the Maserati's surprisingly shitty in-dash GPS and trying to follow the Realtor's vehicle tracker, she got turned around. She panicked a little, then she realized she knew where he was going and that she didn't have to get there the same way.

She punched "Tallahassee" into the GPS and continued.

Just after dawn she hit Florida. And after that Tallahassee. Things started to make sense, and with the aid of the tracker, she picked him up at a grocery store on the south side of town. She saw him exit the store with a sub sandwich and a gallon of filtered water. He drank from the jug and ate the sandwich while looking at a map spread out on the hood of the Escalade. Then he got in and headed south again.

Fifteen minutes after she picked him up again, Hobbs pulled into a tiny used car lot on the edge of town. He was there for twenty minutes, and when he pulled out, it was in an old blue pickup truck with plates that read, "Farm Use."

Following him was harder now, but she didn't have to work at it for long. He drove on for another mile and then pulled into the Palm Court Motor Inn. She drove past and pulled into the strip mall next door. She left the car and walked quickly to where she had a view.

If there ever had been any palm trees at the motor court, it looked as if they had been sold long ago to pay the power bill. Or the water bill. One thing was certain, the money hadn't been used to buy a new coat of paint.

Hobbs stumbled as he came out of the office, and dropped the key as he caught himself. Wellsley could see that this old bastard was going to be sleeping awhile, for sure. She watched him go into room number three and close the blackout curtains.

The strip mall had a prepaid mobile phone store. She bought a Motorola i290, a refurbished candy-bar phone that, instead of a fancy touch screen, sported actual buttons. She also bought a Samsung Galaxy Prevail, a smartphone with a big screen. She signed up for sixteen gigabytes of data and unlimited cell service for three months for both of them. When the salesman, a young black kid in a Cuban shirt, asked her for her address and credit card numbers, she smiled at him and said, "Is it OK if I pay cash? I just moved here."

He upped the price without batting an eye. She laid bills on the counter and said, "Keep the change."

When she got back into the Maserati, she plugged a charger into the cigarette lighter and connected the cheap phone.

She pulled the car around where she could keep an eye on the old truck, just in case. Then she went to work on the phone. It was one thin bar off a full charge. Good enough. Wellsley went into the settings and muted every sound the phone might make.

Then she used the phone's crude web browser to navigate to a site called ZippyMapper. A few painfully awkward clicks with the phone's keypad interface started a download.

Then she turned her attention to the Samsung. She navigated to ZippyMapper using the touch screen, and signed up for a new account using a Tor Mail e-mail. Theoretically the FBI could track it, but it would be very difficult, and they could only really do it if they knew what they were looking for.

When that was done, she activated the software on the Motorola, connected to her account, and waited. It took two minutes before the large display on the Galaxy showed her location. Her ghetto LoJack was open for business.

She drove north, back along the boulevard, until she came to a home improvement warehouse. There she bought a roll of duct tape. She carefully wound tape around the outside of the Motorola until she had doubled its diameter. Then she drove back to the motel.

In the heat of the afternoon, nothing was stirring at the palmless Palm Court Motor Inn. The pickup truck was parked nose-in. She walked in the shade of the balcony above, right to the front of the truck. Then she bent down, maybe tying a shoelace, maybe picking up a dime, and tried to slide the wrapped phone in between the bumper and the frame. Too big. She took two wraps off the duct tape and it wedged in nice and tight.

As she drove away she allowed her guard to slip for a moment. She closed her eyes at the light and let the excitement shiver out of her. A car horn let her know the light had changed. She also needed rest. But there was one more thing she needed to do. This car was about to be the second-hottest vehicle in Florida.

FIVE

Pedro López-Famosa y Fernández, known to his few friends as Perrucho, stared at the expensive green sports car that pulled onto his car lot. This car, he thought, might be worth more than his entire inventory. What were the odds that two such expensive cars driving onto his lot in one day was coincidence? Zero, thought Perrucho.

The cars that Perrucho sold were, of course, crap. Sold to people who could not, or would not, pay. The kind of people who spent the money that should have been their car payment on renting ridiculous wheels at exorbitant rates. Whatever they had left over would go to purchasing used tires.

It was good for business that he did not identify with the creatures he called his customers. That kept the conscience pure and the interest rates high, and made it easy for Perrucho to take the cars back. But, as this blond woman in a suit entered his tiny office, he realized he might understand this *gringa* less than he understood his usual customers. For a second he thought she might be a cop, but a cop in that car? Could not be. And a cop who looked like that? It was the kind of thing that could make a man like Perrucho pray for the handcuffs, but not the squad car.

"Can I help you?" Perrucho asked, wearing his most professional smile.

"I've got a trade-in, and a friend of mine told me you could help me out."

"Señora? You mean that beautiful car? I do not know what friend we could have in common, but he or she was very badly mistaken. I would not know what to do with such an expensive car. I cannot sell it to my customers. They are all too poor. Besides, none of my cars would be suitable for your luxurious tastes."

The woman frowned. "But my friend was just here, he told me he got a very good deal."

"I have made no deals today, I am sorry. Perhaps you mean Flaco's place? His place is a little further down," he said with a smile. "Besides, for a deal such as that, there is much paperwork. And I do not even have the forms. I sell cars, I do not buy them."

The blond woman said, "What I am looking for is an exchange."

"What you are suggesting sounds like it would be very illegal," said Perrucho, having fun with it. "I do not think I could do something like that. Señora, my nerves, they are not so good."

The woman reached into her pocket and pulled out her FBI ID and badge. "Then how about if I place you under arrest?"

Perrucho laughed and leaned forward in his chair. He leaned across the desk and presented his hands. "Please, put me in the cuffs. Because I ask myself. If you are here to arrest me, then why do you not have backup?"

The woman said nothing.

"I think you are in more trouble than I am. If someone is looking for that fancy car, then, señorita, you need me more than I need you."

The blond woman had no response to this. She stood there blinking back tears. Perrucho thought they were tears of weakness and frustration. Exhaustion at the end of a long and difficult road. Leverage.

"I do have an offer for you. If you can buy one of my cars for the bargain price of twenty thousand dollars, then I will take the Maserati and dispose of it quietly. How does that sound to you?"

"I don't..."

"I know, I know," said Perrucho, holding up a hand. "You don't have the money. And there are many, many excuses for this. Believe me, I have heard them all. And I sympathize. I am not a man without a heart. So I tell you what I will do. I will give you a five-thousand-dollar discount if you let me see those breasts of yours."

The blonde grew red in the face. She started to speak, but he cut her off again.

"But wait, for you, a special price, ten thousand dollars to solve all of your problems if you strip naked in this office, right now. And I want you to know, that is a better deal than I gave your friend. Of course, you are free to reject my deal. But then I am afraid that, law-abiding citizen that I am, I would have to call the police and report such strange behavior."

SIX

When she was done, Wellsley flipped the Closed sign, locked the door, and went through Perrucho's pockets. Even though that filthy, patriarchal prick had deserved it, she avoided looking at the work she had done. The hole in his face was small, but the soft, expanding bullet had torn the back of his head almost completely off. She repositioned a poster on the wall to cover the splatter and bits of hair.

In his pockets she found a Mercedes key fob and a wallet. There were $200 in cash and no family pictures. Yeah, she thought, this one she could probably get away with. Even if somebody called it in, police departments waited seventy-two hours before they would classify someone as a missing person. And how long would it be before somebody missed this greasy prick?

A week on the outside? But she was sure she wouldn't need that. She'd get the money and be gone. South, over the border from Texas somewhere. The north of Mexico wouldn't be a good place to hang out, but Cabo San Lucas would be fine for a blond American girl. And from there Panama, where a second passport was easy to get. Especially if you were willing to buy property.

She knew how and where money was laundered. And she knew to broker small deals and not take any chances. Hiding her identity and cleaning the money would be a full-time job for a while, but it would pay well. She might have already been done with it if she had gotten the money the first time. And having a hurricane to cover her tracks, that would have been perfect.

As she drove away in Perrucho's battered old Mercedes—with what was left of Perrucho in the trunk—she told herself that it would be fine. It would all be fine, if she took it slow and got it right this time. She'd get away, and nobody would ever have her under their thumb again.

She checked the GPS tracker on her phone. Hobbs was still at the motor court. Now all she had to do was wait.

She got a room at the motor court, number twelve, across the horseshoe from where Hobbs was. She set an alarm for three thirty in the morning and tried to get some sleep. But she was too jittery to get to sleep. She thought about kicking the old man's door in, pistol-whipping him, and forcing him to take her to the money. Better to let him lead her unthinkingly. That way he couldn't lie.

When three thirty rolled around, the blue truck was still there. She watched for a little over two hours. Then she fell asleep in the chair. When she woke up the truck was gone. Her heart raced, and she cursed her weakness. But the tracker still had him. Three miles south on 319.

She caught up with him in Medart. The truck was parked at a dive center, and a young kid was helping him load gear into the back of the truck. She saw him moving slowly as she drove by, and turned her head away as she passed. She didn't think she'd have any problem taking care of this one old man. He looked dog tired and it wasn't even ten in the morning. She felt like a lioness, stalking the weakest member of the herd.

He headed west, following the right angle of US Route 319. The afternoon sun was blinding through the windshield, and the air conditioner in the Mercedes strained. If this took too much longer, she thought, Perrucho was going to start to smell.

When Hobbs pulled off, she missed it. She couldn't see anything with that sun. It wasn't until she had gotten up onto the long bridge that she realized he must have taken the small dirt turnout before. As the monotonous length of the bridge shrank before her, she checked the GPS. Three pings in a row showed the car stopped back at the foot of the bridge. This must be it.

She doubled back, then back again. She parked the Mercedes over half a mile before the turnout and continued on foot. She told the trunk, "Wait here," and chuckled to herself at her gallows humor. Why shouldn't she be happy, she tried to convince herself, she was about to be rich.

She dogtrotted down the side of the road. No cars passed in either direction. A good sign. When she got to the turnout, the road sloped down and turned left sharply. The road was hemmed in by the low vegetation of the brackish marsh. As she drew her weapon, she felt as if she were entering a tunnel.

She thought of the words *Freeze, FBI*, shouted, cheesy, like in the movies. She considered how false those words had become for her—she having crossed way, way over to the wrong side of the law—but she would yell them, if she thought they would do any good. She was done taking chances. Her whole life the guys—the bad guys, were there any other kind?—had been winning, and she was sick of it. Now she was going to get hers.

She realized, with disappointment, that she couldn't shoot to kill. She needed him alive, just in case this wasn't where the money was.

She saw that the truck was backed up next to the concrete edge of the bridge footing. Hobbs was nowhere in sight. She advanced cautiously. She heard a sound and froze until she could identify it. Bubbles. It was bubbles.

At the water's edge was a steady stream of bubbles coming up from a scuba rig. They made the long, brilliant sunlight of the afternoon dance on the surface of the water. He must be down there, right now. All she had to do was wait until he came up. Verify that the money was down there, then shoot him and take the scuba gear for herself. All she needed now was a little patience.

She relaxed and held the pistol by her side. Wellsley hadn't realized how tightly she had been gripping it. A rookie mistake. She passed the gun to her left hand and flexed her fingers. It felt good and bad all at the same time. Then…

SEVEN

Hobbs slept like a dead man and woke with a powerful hunger. He pissed for what felt like twenty minutes, pain shooting through his bladder. He felt ossified by old age and abuse. He ate breakfast in the diner next to the hotel. The eggs were good, the coffee was terrible.

The heat was off enough that he could take it slow. The Escalade was the most stolen car in the United States. He had paid $30,000 to get rid of it. The guy would either chop it for parts, or put it on a boat and sell it overseas. He doubted anybody would ever find it. Which made that rattly old pickup truck safe as houses. Sure, there was a chance the guy would report it as stolen to get the insurance money, but it wouldn't be worth the hassle or the heat. Car dealers defrauding insurance companies was an old racket, and even filing an honest claim brought suspicion.

As long as that pickup truck kept running, he was home free. He smiled and thought about returning to Grace. About sleeping for a whole day in their bed with the feather pillows and the green comforter with the leaf pattern that he had hated so much at first. Then napping the following day—all day—in the hammock. And never taking a job again.

He caught himself smiling and shook it off. He touched the wound in his side to remind himself. This was a job. Maybe the end of a job, but a job all the same. Get careless, get dead. There had been enough mistakes for one job.

He saw Alan's face for an instant. Bright and cocky. Then he saw the image of the kid's corpse jumping in the rain as the bullet went through his head. And Hurlocker, that rough old bastard. A shame that he was dead, but not a tragedy. Not the same as the kid. That kid had had his whole life before him.

He walked back to the motor court and watched very carefully for a while. He didn't see anything, but that didn't calm his nerves any. He put the key into the truck's ignition and was grateful when it started. He headed south.

He thought of Grace. He closed his eyes and he could see her face, with sunlight on it. Not the glaring tropical burn of the Florida sun, but the clean, cool sun of late summer filtered through the leaves of tall green trees.

He made Wellsley at the dive shop, as the kid was loading up the tanks. Wide eyes and a flash of short blond hair in a silver Mercedes that drove by just a little too slowly. Never look directly at someone you are following. Sometimes they feel the eyes, even when they aren't looking for them.

He remembered that Mercedes from Perrucho's car lot. Parked right out in front. Perrucho had been proud of it. How had she tracked him? Could Hobbs have done the same if the roles had been reversed? What had happened to Perrucho?

He didn't care. He closed his eyes and could see her, standing under the tungsten light as the ocean roared and the rain came down. Her short hair plastered to her skull, fear and greed gleaming in her wild eyes.

Stupid girl. She had done it the wrong way. She had to be new. As corrupt as the FBI was, she could have found people to go in on it with her. Heist the heister. The second-oldest scam in the book. The easiest way was to underreport the money recovered. Hell, the FBI could even drop the serial numbers of marked bills from its database. It had been in on scams like this since Dillinger. Long before the civil asset forfeiture racket. Hell, when you got right down to it, that's how the whole thing started. Wasn't the American Revolution a heist?

An honest criminal couldn't make a living anymore. But crooked cops sure were a growth industry.

He thought of three ways to lose her and all the reasons he should. He was tired. He was slow. He was old.

Alan bleeding to death on the sand.

He wanted this to be over. More than he could remember ever wanting a job to be over. He wanted to walk away. But instead added an extra three tanks. And a speargun.

"Don't let them game wardens find you using that in freshwater. You'll be in a mess of trouble then," said the guy at the dive shop.

He continued to the bridge. That crooked FBI agent hung way back, but the afternoon sunlight glinted off the silver car as if it were a signaling mirror every time it came into view. Jesus Christ, she was green. He felt even worse about having let her get the better of him.

Around a curve he gave the rattly old pickup all it was worth to stretch the distance between them. He skidded into the turnoff before she came into sight. He jumped out of the truck, his knee buckling painfully, and limped up to the road. He stepped into the brush and listened to her car roar past and onto the bridge. No turnaround in the middle of that long span. That should give him the time he needed.

He pulled the truck up to the foot of the bridge and worked quickly. Hobbs hauled a tank from the back of the truck and dragged it to the edge of the river. Then he opened the valve until he heard the first rush of air. With all the strength he could muster, he heaved it out into the river. It sank like a stone, sending up a quiet trail of bubbles.

Then he grabbed the speargun out of the bed of the truck and grunted as he pulled the three-ply surgical tubing to the catch. He laid one of the three-pointed, barbed spears into the track. It was a grisly weapon. A gun would be cleaner and more professional. But he did not have a gun. And even though it was unprofessional, he didn't want this to be clean.

He test-fired at the concrete bridge abutment ten feet away. The spear dropped hard, but it hit with such force the fiberglass shaft broke into two pieces. Good enough.

He reloaded the spear gun, then threw the pieces of the broken spear into the river. Then he stepped into the underbrush, lined up on the bubbles, and lay down. Not long after he settled, he heard footsteps coming down the dirt road. Slow and careful, but they were there.

He willed himself not to turn his head and look. He was lying on his belly, and his field of fire was set. The only way this would work would be if she came into his kill zone. The fiberglass fragments from the shattered spear caused his hand to itch. He did not scratch it.

He heard her moving by the truck. Then he heard nothing. From the left of his field of vision, she edged into view. He allowed just his eyes to move so he could see her better. It was only a slight improvement, as his nose now blocked the view from his right eye. He closed his eye.

She was holding her gun in the classic Weaver stance all law enforcement was taught. It was a stupid way to hold a gun when you were working on your own. Too easy to get tunnel vision. And what if they were behind you? It took too long to turn. Worst of all, it was a physical advertisement, as subtle as a giant neon sign flashing, "I have a gun! I have a gun!"

She edged up to the water and looked at the bubbles. Now she was directly in his line of fire. He saw her shoulders relax. She switched the gun to her left hand. Hobbs fired.

The spear seemed to fly slowly, comically slowly, toward Wellsley. Hobbs knew it was just the weirdness of adrenaline.

When the barbed spear hit, it slid right through her suit jacket, under her rib and out her belly. She gasped and fell forward on her knees.

Hobbs was up and moving, forcing himself to move fast, but not to rush with excitement. Before Wellsley could turn, he hit her with the handle of the spear gun and she went out.

EIGHT

When Wellsley woke she was lying on her side. She tried to roll and the spear levered against the ground, wrenching into her guts. She cried out and opened her eyes.

"Oh God!" she said, as she reached for the spear protruding from her belly.

"I wouldn't," said Hobbs.

She turned her head and was able to see Hobbs, lashing three air tanks together. She kicked at him, feebly, and winced as the pain radiated outward from her stomach. "I'm a goddamned FBI agent. And backup is coming," she said.

"Goddamned," said Hobbs, agreeing. He squinted against the sunset and looked up and down the river. Empty. A car roared past on the bridge above. It was a lonely sound. Hobbs bent to pick up a line and made it fast to the tanks.

"What are you going to do to me?" asked Wellsley.

"I'm going to show you where the money is," said Hobbs. And he kicked the tanks into the water. The rope snapped tight and Wellsley felt herself being dragged backward by her ankle. She clawed at the grass and the earth, trying to arrest her progress, but the weight of the tanks dragged against her. The barbs caught in her flesh and the spear wrenched her organs. She gasped in pain, ripping at the grasses and small trees growing by the side of the road. A small shrub held.

Hobbs stepped around her and leaned up against the pickup truck to watch.

"Fuck you. Fuck you," said Wellsley. "I'm going to fucking kill you."

"You're not going to beg for your life?"

"Fucking kill you," said Wellsley.

"Not going to beg me to kill you?"

"Fuck you."

"OK," said Hobbs, pulling her pistol from his belt. He popped the clip and looked at it. He showed it to her. "Full," he said, laying the weapon on the ground six feet in front of her. Just at the edge of her own shadow, cast by the setting sun.

Hobbs said, "I'm going to go get the Mercedes and drive it back here. If you get to the pistol, you can try to shoot me."

Then Hobbs walked away without looking back. He heard scrabbling in the dirt, Wellsley grunting in pain. He didn't like this kind of thing, but felt, somehow, that he owed it to the kid.

He walked the half mile back to the Mercedes. By the time he got there, the sun was down and the light of day had faded to a redness in the west. He sat in the car and did not start it until well after the first stars had come out.

He drove the Mercedes back to the bridge slowly, almost missing the turnoff in the dark. In the headlights he saw the handgun still lying in the road. He got out and picked it up.

In the sand he could see her blood and read her struggle. She had clawed forward, maybe a foot. Who knew how many times she had gone back and forth. He saw shredded fingernails on the concrete footing of the bridge. He threw the pistol in after her.

He rolled all the windows down in the Mercedes. Then he rolled it into the river and watched it sink.

NINE

Broyles was drunk. He had just come home from a dinner on an energy company's expense account, and very expensive bourbon was percolating through his much-abused liver. His thoughts turned to Darlene, asleep upstairs, and he regretted his liquor-limp dick. But that was no impediment to a man with a bottle of little blue pills.

He staggered through the house to the wood-paneled room that he called his study, but that was really nothing more than an office filled with books he had never read. There he concealed his Viagra from his wife. Of course, she knew, but both of them were grifters enough to know that there was no profit in destroying this pointless con of a vain old man.

When he turned on the lights, Broyles saw Hobbs sitting in his favorite chair.

"Jesus Christ!" he said, swaying as he tried to find a handle on the moment. "Hobbs. I had given you up for dead." He squinted and realized how bad Hobbs looked. He muttered, "And you may yet be," as he poured himself into an armchair that faced the desk. He asked, "Where's the money?"

"Where I left it. Soaking in an armored car under the east side of the bridge over the Sopchoppy River. US Route 319. I dumped a crooked FBI agent and a car on top. But it's all there."

"Well?" Broyles asked, shaking his chin wattle in confusion. "When are you going to go get it?"

"I quit."

"You can't quit. There's millions of dollars down there."

"Find somebody else. I'm here to tell you I quit."

"But what about your share? What about your crew? Don't they expect to be paid?"

"They're all dead."

"Jesus, Hobbs! What went wrong?"

Hobbs told him.

"My God."

Hobbs got up.

"Hobbs, when I recover it, I will save you a share."

"Sure," said Hobbs. And they smiled, both knowing that it was a lie.

TEN

Hobbs drove the pickup into the garage and pulled the door down behind him. As he straightened to look at himself in the rearview mirror, a pain shot through his ribs. His face was pale, and pools of blood in the whites of his eyes seemed the most substantial thing about him. Sixty, going on 160.

As he walked from the garage to the house, the quiet lapping of the lake made him uneasy.

He entered through the side door and heard music coming from the deck. Grace would be there, enjoying the last warmth of the day, reading a novel for diversion. It wouldn't be a thriller, though. She never read those when he was away. She worried enough, she said, without fertilizing her imagination.

He wanted sunglasses. He knew how old and tired he must look. He wanted to spare her the shock of it. He wanted to take all the suffering for himself. For the first time, he recognized that this desire was love but could not shape this understanding into words.

He poured himself two fingers of Scotch and carried it to the glass door. From where she lay, he could see only her large sun hat and the bottoms of her legs. Just like the rest of her, her calves and feet still looked good to him after all these years.

He put the glass down on a side table and opened the door. She looked up, pretending she was still reading her book. Then she couldn't pretend anymore. She rushed to his arms.

As they held each other, tears poured down his cheeks in silence. He was ashamed at his weeping, but that made him weep all the more.

After a while, she asked, "What is it?"

"I'm done."

ABOUT THE AUTHOR

Patrick E. McLean is an award-winning author and narrator who never writes anything straight down the line. His work includes the Parsec Award–winning How to Succeed in Evil series and *The Merchant Adventurer*.

Among his influences, Patrick cites such irreconcilables as Richard Stark, Douglas Adams, Mark Helprin, Terry Pratchett, S. J. Perelman, H. L. Mencken, Hafez, Homer, Georges Simenon, and Jorge Luis Borges.

Made in the USA
Lexington, KY
25 April 2017